To save us all

from

Satan's power

To save us all

from

Satan's power

Kenn Grimes

Deer Lake Publishing
Boyne City, Michigan

© Copyright 2021 by Kenn Grimes

Publisher
Deer Lake Press
715 E. Deer Lake Rd.
Boyne City, Michigan, 49712
deerlakepress@aol.com

ISBN 978-0-9860020-2-1
Soft cover
First Edition

Contact the author at kenngrimesauthor@aol.com

Other books by

KENN GRIMES

CHAPTER ONE

Beer in one hand, a cigarette in the other, Darren O'Shea paced the floor of the tiny kitchen. His eyes never left Alice, who sat at a rickety wooden table pock-marked by dark burn stains, a beer in front of her.

Like Darren, she held a cigarette in her hand.

She was obviously drunk.

At seventeen she had been a beautiful woman, skin a deep-brown chocolate.

Despite the fact Darren, an Irish Catholic from the small Mississippi town of Gilbert's Place, loathed African-Americans, he fell in love with her at first sight, and they'd been married within a month. He was twenty-four.

Now, at thirty-two, time, alcohol and cigarettes had taken their toll on his wife. The extra fifty pounds she'd added over the years hadn't helped.

But Darren still loved her.

Almost as much as he loved the prospect of finally being rich.

"I'm rich," he said, matter-of-factly. His head bobbed up and down as if affirming the point. "Son-of-a-bitch, I'm finally rich!"

"What do you mean, you're rich?" asked Alice, slurring the words.

"Lottery my ass! That two grand you been getting every month has been coming from that asshole."

Alice lowered her head. "I shouldn't have said nothing. I shouldn't have told you Patty ain't your kid."

"Hell, I always figured Patty wasn't mine. But now the son-of-a-bitch is going to pay me a lot more than the two gees he's been sending you."

"But . . . but I didn't tell you who he was so you could get money out of him."

"Yeah, you always did run off at the mouth when you got sloshed. And I don't give a shit why you told me. You told me. Now the bastard's going to pay through the nose."

"But Darren—"

"Shut up, Alice!" shouted Darren.

He slapped her across the mouth, sending her tumbling off the chair. "Just shut up! You been getting that fucking money all these years. Now it's my turn."

Darren looked around the kitchen, at the outdated appliances, the faded wallpaper, and the hole in one corner of the ceiling. He dropped his cigarette onto the linoleum floor and squashed it with the toe of his boot.

Alice managed to right herself to where her arms and head rested on the table.

"First thing we're going to do is move out of this shithole," said Darren. He went to the refrigerator, opened it, reached in, and grabbed another beer.

*****

Darren leaned back against the faded, crumbling, brick wall of the warehouse. A half-smoked cigarette dangled from his lips. It was the same building where he'd worked for fourteen years after getting out of the army until the company decided four years ago to outsource its manufacturing facilities to Southeast Asia. Now the structure stood empty, like all the others around it an embodiment of the whole neighborhood.

He knew the area would be deserted.

He watched as a shiny, silver Lexus LX 470 pulled up, its headlights playing over the building's shuttered windows and doors.

Without turning off the engine or dimming the lights, the driver opened the door, got out, and approached Darren.

The man towered over Darren by a good six inches. It was apparent he had money and enjoyed expensive things, not only from the automobile he'd arrived in but from the cashmere overcoat he wore.

"So you're Patty's daddy," said Darren. He put the cigarette out on the side of the building and stepped forward. "Just so's you know, there's been a change of plans. That hundred grand you brought tonight? That's just the first installment. It's going to cost you five gees a month from now on, plus the two you been sending Alice."

The man smiled and stuck a hand into his coat pocket. "You're right about one thing, you little shit. There has been a change of plans."

When he brought the hand back out of his pocket, it held a Baretta 92FS. He pointed it at Darren and fired once.

A look of shock covered Darren's face. He staggered backward and collapsed against the wall. A dark red stain spread over the white shirt visible under his open windbreaker.

He slumped to the ground, a look of disbelief in his eyes.

The man walked toward Darren and stood over him for a moment, admiring his handiwork. Then he fired a second time, the bullet entering directly between Darren's still open eyes.

The man smiled again, removed the silencer from the barrel of the gun, casually placed both pieces back into his coat pocket, returned to the car, and drove off.

CHAPTER TWO
(thirty-six days until the Presidential election)

In the eighteen years since the still-unsolved murder of Darren O'Shea, America, like the rest of the world, had changed in ways both large and small.

Computers were smaller and more powerful, replaced in many cases by iPads and smartphones, which themselves had gotten smaller, then larger again. Texting, tweeting, and Instagrams, became the preferred forms of communicating and disseminating information. Smartwatches were all the rage as were gigantic flat-screen television sets that displayed life-size images of football players doing their best to incapacitate their opponents.

Facebook made it possible for everyone in the world to now know what one ate for breakfast and Google put the entire globe's knowledge at a person's fingertips. If you needed something, you went to Amazon, not the nearby grocery store—if there even was one anymore.

Climate change had become an even hotter topic, made all the more relevant by a significant increase in average world temperature and sea levels, violent weather—storms, including hurricanes, tornados, blizzards—along with catastrophic droughts, and floods.

A pandemic that had raged for over a year had ultimately been brought under control.

And while the United States continued to be the world's one true superpower, it now found a new foe hard on its heels: China.

Hunger was still a way of life around the globe, with over ten percent of its seven and a half billion people undernourished.

The war on terror initiated after the September 11, 2001 attack on the United States was still being waged, both in the United States and countries around the world.

The polarization of the United States Congress that saw its beginnings in the 1970s had grown into a full-blown chasm between the left and right, where civility no longer was the standard of the day.

Democrats ruled the Senate, while Republicans held forth in the House.

The nation's Supreme Court had seen a dramatic shift—some called it a nose-dive—to the right, while the executive branch—namely the President—attempted to exert its power and influence more and more.

All of which rendered the upcoming general election so much more important than anyone could have imagined.

*****

Jeanette Evans had been Bobby Winslow's girl Friday ever since he'd been elected a U. S. Senator from California. When he became governor of that same state four years ago she followed him to Sacramento. Secretary, confidant, and gatekeeper, she was as close to him as anyone, including Ku´ualoha, Bobby's partner of eleven years.

Fifty-something and prim almost to a fault, she ran her boss's office with a firm hand. Her work area was simply furnished with no more than the bare necessities: a desk, chair, computer, printer, fax machine, and a four-drawer file cabinet. In one corner, under a photograph of the President of the United States, Robert Winslow, was a second chair for the occasional visitor who might drop by. In another corner, a small stand held a coffee pot, a stack of Styrofoam cups, and a dish of artificial creamers, sweeteners, and wooden stirrers.

As usual, Jeanette was at her desk, typing, when Bobby entered.

Forty-two, and several inches shy of six feet, Bobby Winslow sported a body that had enjoyed way too many Krispy Kreme doughnuts in its time. Today he appeared with two full Starbucks coffee cups—and a bag of the aforementioned doughnuts.

"Good morning, Jeanette," he said, a brightness in his tone.

"Good morning, Governor," said Jeanette without looking up.

Bobby set one of the cups and the bag of doughnuts on Jeanette's desk. She glanced at them but continued typing.

"What's the occasion?" she asked.

"Nothing special; I woke up this morning thinking what a great job you do and how much I appreciate you."

A smile almost escaped Jeanette's lips.

"And?"

"That's it; nothing more."

"Then thank you very much. Even though you know I don't need them."

"Are you kidding?" said Bobby. "You have the best-looking body of any forty-year-old woman I know."

"And you *also* know that I'm fifty-two."

Bobby faked a surprised look. "Really? In that case, you have the best-looking body of any fifty-two-year-old woman I know."

"Not that you spend much time looking at women's bodies," said Jeanette.

Bobby chuckled. His sexual orientation was no secret.

"Kevin in yet?" he asked.

"Here when I arrived."

Bobby headed for his office. "I swear, sometimes I think the guy must sleep here." He stopped and turned around. "Jeanette, how many years have you worked for me?"

"Twelve, sir, going on thirteen."

"And in all those years, how many times have I asked you to call me Bobby, instead of Senator or Governor?"

"One hundred and fifty-nine . . . Governor."

This time Jeanette actually smiled.

Bobby shook his head and entered his office.

"Paper's on your desk," said Jeanette over her shoulder.

*****

Bobby's office was more sparsely furnished than Jeanette's if that were possible. There were no photographs, nor any other pictures for that matter. The only thing that broke the white starkness of the walls was a fifty-two-inch flat-screen TV.

He'd just finished *The Sacramento Bee* sports section when Kevin Sperling, his Chief of Staff rushed in. Bobby looked up.

"Hey, Kevin, good morn—"

"You've got to see this," interrupted Kevin, hurrying over to the TV and turning it on.

Bobby swiveled in his chair toward the screen. Aaron Brody, a news analyst for KCRA was on the air.

"This breaking news just in; Gerald McClaren, the Democratic candidate for president, is dead at the age of fifty-three. Senator McClaren was discovered by his aide in his hotel room this morning in Atlanta. It is believed the senator suffered a heart attack."

Bobby leaned back in his chair, a look of astonishment on his face. "My God!" he muttered.

Brody continued. "According to the senator's campaign manager, Matt Overstreet, Senator McClaren had no history of any heart condition. It is not known at this time how the senator's death will affect the upcoming election, scheduled for five weeks from tomorrow. We will bring you additional news as it becomes available."

"I can't believe this is happening again," said Kevin, muting the TV.

"You mean like four years ago?"

"Yeah. Your dad wouldn't be in office today if that idiot, Burger, hadn't knocked up his fourteen-year-old cousin."

"That *was* bad timing, wasn't it?—the whole affair becoming public two weeks before the election. After that, the poor sucker didn't stand a chance."

"And your daddy won every state."

"Including Burger's home state."

"Now it's going to happen again," said Kevin.

A disgusted look on his face, he plopped down onto the one other chair in the office.

The phone on Bobby's desk rang. He pushed a button, putting the phone on speaker. "Who is it, Jeanette?" he asked.

"Everybody and his brother," came Jeanette's voice over the intercom.

"Okay, choose the most important one. I'll take it first. See how many of the rest you can get rid of."

"Yes, sir. Guess you heard the news."

"Kevin and I just saw the report."

*****

Dressed in a Dallas Cowboys tee shirt and sweat pants, Robert Winslow rode a stationary bike set up in one corner of a room filled with exercise equipment. Sixty-five-years old, tall, and trim, with movie-star looks, he was in great shape. As he pedaled, he was engrossed in the book lying open before him: *Islamic World Domination, Fact or Fiction?*

More formally attired in a suit, as he almost always was, Robert's personal aide, Jamie Inskeep, stood by the window and gazed out at the nearby St. Louis Gateway Arch. In his mid-thirties, Jamie had been with Robert for eleven years, the first four as an aide in Robert's second term as Governor of Texas.

When that came to an end, Robert took Jamie with him when he accepted a partnership in a large, prestigious Dallas law firm, and later when he won his first term of office as President of the United States.

Jamie's hope had been that Robert would choose him to be his new Chief of Staff. Though it didn't happen, as far as Jamie was concerned, Robert Winslow walked on water. He'd do anything for him.

This was Jamie's second Presidential campaign with Robert. St. Louis was the fourth stop on the tour, following rallies in Chattanooga, Sarasota, and Baton Rouge. After tonight's speech at the annual AAW convention, they were scheduled to leave tomorrow for Seattle where Robert was to address the national NAACP convention. Five more stops in three days followed.

Robert laid the book aside and took the TV remote. "Jamie, get me a Bloody Mary."

In the adjoining room of the suite, Robert's wife, Wilma, sat at a dressing table, mechanically running a brush through her hair. She laid the brush on the table next to a glass filled with scotch. A half-empty bottle sat nearby. She smoothed back the graying, thinning hair from her face, then leaned in toward the mirror, studying the lines under her eyes.

And frowned.

Forty pounds overweight and seven years older than her husband, Wilma looked more like fifteen years his senior.

She knew when he'd first begun to court her forty-four years ago she was no match for him in the looks department. He was handsome, tall and muscular, a former high school football and basketball player. She was short and plump, even then; and older than he. She knew much of the attraction she held for him had to do with her family's considerable fortune.

She hadn't cared.

Four years at the exclusive girls' school, Our Lady of Holy Cross College, offered little opportunity to meet eligible bachelors. And since the school was located in New Orleans, where she and her parents lived, they insisted she continue to reside at home, and not in a dorm.

If Robert hadn't come along that Mardi Gras and met her at the ball at the Clarendon Plantation she might still be unmarried. Her parents evidently felt the same way when they allowed their daughter to wed this younger man, a Baptist no less, in a non-Catholic church ceremony over the objections of their parish priest.

What Wilma and Robert had now was not so much a marriage as an arrangement. Yes, she was the First Lady of the United States and traveled with him on many, though not all, of his trips, both domestic and abroad. She had people to wait on her and take care of her. Together she and Robert had what she considered a remarkable son, even if Robert would have nothing to do with him because he was gay—and a Democrat, to boot.

Then there was the booze: an unending supply of alcohol, whatever her heart desired. If not for that, life would have been unbearable.

What *was* lacking was intimacy and affection. It had been years since they had made love, though she knew he found his needs satisfied elsewhere.

She dreaded the thought of another four years in the White House. She wasn't sure she could make it.

She heard Robert's voice from the other room.

"Son-of-a-bitch! Wilma!"

Wilma jumped up and rushed into the next room. Robert had stopped pedaling but still sat astride the bike.

"Robert, what—?"

"Shut up and watch this," Robert said as he wiped his face with a towel and pointed to the TV. "*Look* at this. *Son*-of-a-bitch! I do believe lighting has struck twice!"

The three of them watched while the announcer rapidly spat out the breaking news.

"Senator McClaren was discovered early this morning by his aide, Lydia Morgan. First indication is that the senator suffered a massive heart attack. He was scheduled to speak today at the American Legion Convention."

Wilma looked at Robert. "Jerry? Is he okay?"

"Okay? Hell, no, he's not okay! The sucker's dead! Kicked the bucket. Bought the farm. You know what this means?"

Wilma shrugged.

"It means I've got the election sewed up. Those fucking Democrats can't come up with anyone else at this late date to take McClaren's place. Nobody who could beat me, anyway."

"What about Tom Forrester?" asked Jamie.

"Forrester? Ha! That over the hill fossil could never get enough votes. I've got another four years in the bag!"

Wilma flinched but recovered enough to walk over and kiss Robert on the cheek. "I'm happy for you, dear," she said.

"Four more years. Now I can put my plan in operation. They'll remember Robert Winslow now, by God!"

"That's nice, dear," said Wilma, seemingly unimpressed.

Robert looked at her. "You don't understand any of this, do you? You have no idea the magnitude of what I'm about to undertake."

"I . . . I guess not," Wilma stuttered. "What is it?"

Robert waved his hand dismissively at Wilma and shook his head. "Never mind; Jamie, get Nate in here."

CHAPTER THREE

A TV on top of an old dresser and a mattress on the floor on which Muhammad and P.J. were engaged in sex were the extent of the furnishings the room held.

A thirty-year-old light-skinned African American, P.J. Little was strikingly beautiful, winsome and petite, no more than a whisper. She was married when she met Muhammad nine years ago at the club where his band was playing. They'd hit it off immediately and the next day she'd filed for divorce. Not willing to make the same mistake twice, she'd rebuffed his offer of marriage three times since, though they now lived together with Meow, their cat.

Right now Meow, extremely jealous of Muhammad, was locked outside the bedroom.

Like P.J., Muhammad was a light-skinned African-American, two months older than her. A good foot taller than P.J., he was as handsome as she was beautiful.

In spite of his name, he was definitely not Arab.

Suddenly P.J. was distracted by something on the TV. She turned her head to watch.

"Muhammad, wait—stop!" she said.

"Why, what is it?"

"I don't fucking believe it! He's dead?"

"Who's dead?"

14

P.J. pushed Muhammad off of her. "Listen."

". . . died of a heart attack. McClaren was fifty-three."

Muhammad sat straight up. "McClaren? Shit! You know what this means?"

P.J. shook her head, a disgusted look on her face. "Don't tell me—four more years of that idiot in the White House."

"Four more fucking years," Muhammad added, disbelief in his voice.

"You think McClaren could have beat him?"

"Are you kidding? In a heartbeat! Nobody wants that son-of-a-bitch back in office."

"That's not quite true."

"Oh, okay. The ones who are getting rich off that fucking war in Guinea this dumbass started last year."

P.J. jumped up.

"P.J.? Where you going?"

"I have to go."

"Where?"

"The paper. This is a big story."

"Yeah, but it's already broken. What are you going to do?"

P.J. threw on a sweatshirt and a pair of jeans and slipped into a pair of moccasins. "I don't know." She hurried to the door and blew a kiss to Muhammad. "Something; I'll see you later."

*****

The sign on the door read 'John Clancy, Editor.'

Inside, the office was cluttered with newspapers and other odds and ends. The owner of the title on the door sat at a desk as messy as the rest of the room. A copy of his company's paper, the *Washington Eagle*, lay open in front of him.

In his late fifties, heavy-set, wearing a white shirt open at the neck with an untied tie draped around it, Clancy sat in an old-fashioned, dilapidated wooden swivel chair, something the Smithsonian might have disposed of. He took a swig of coffee from a mug that enjoyed no more than an occasional rinsing.

A graduate of the School of Communications at American University, P.J. had been hired almost immediately by the paper as an intern and 'gopher.' Within eight years she had worked her way up to a position as an investigative reporter.

She stood facing Clancy, leaning over, her hands resting on his desk. "There's got to be some way to stop this son-of-a-bitch. There's no way we can take four more years of him."

"You got any ideas?" asked Clancy. "'Cause I ain't got a fucking clue how to do it."

"It's no secret the sucker has trouble keeping his pants on," said P.J., sitting down. "And there've been rumors ever since he got into office his hands aren't all that lily-white."

"Maybe," said Clancy. "But nobody's been able to pin anything on him yet."

"I know there's a story here somewhere, and I'm going to find it."

"What do you have in mind?"

P.J. shrugged. "I haven't the faintest clue."

QUINCY'S STORY: CHAPTER I

The last time I saw my mother she was being held at the Los Angeles County Jail.

I was five years old and my father told me later she'd been arrested for prostitution.

He also told me that two days after I visited her, she was stabbed to death by another inmate.

He said he felt responsible for her death. My father was a police officer; he was the one who arrested my mother and had her thrown in jail.

He said she was a drug addict—crack. He'd refused to give her money to buy the drugs and she had turned to the street. He couldn't get her to quit. So he arrested her. He hoped being thrown in jail might make her stop.

I guess it did.

Because, as I said, she got stabbed.

And she died.

Like so many other people I have known.

*****

Growing up in South-Central Los Angeles in the eighties was a matter of life and death—literally.

My three best friends when I was a kid were Coco, Elliott, and Turdy—the latter of whose real name was Lester.

Coco and Elliott were three years older than me; Turdy, two.

The three of them were members of a gang called the Scarabs. Most of the gang members ranged in age from ten to their early twenties. Each sported a tattoo of a beetle on the side of his neck. My friends had tried to get me to join from the time I was nine years old. But I wouldn't. The fact my father was a cop had a lot to do with it. Besides, I liked living too much. And by that, I mean as opposed to dying.

Anyway, by the time I was fourteen, Coco, Elliott, and Turdy were all dead; shot to death by rival gang members.

They weren't old enough to legally buy cigarettes or booze or guns or drive a car.

Although they had done all those things.

Kids grew up fast in my neighborhood.

My friends had all been killed by brothers—other blacks for those who don't know what the term 'brothers' means in our culture.

But it was the white man we feared more, especially cops; my father notwithstanding.

Not only could they arrest us, they could beat us and, on occasion, even kill us, almost with impunity. Not to mention the constant harassment.

I don't know how many times I was stopped by a cop and questioned: *What was I doing? What was I doing here? What did I have in my pocket? Why wasn't I in school?*

When I answered that last question by telling the officer there was no school that day—that it was a teacher's workday—he said I was probably too stupid to learn anything even if I was in school, that us niggers would be better off back in the jungle where we came from.

18

Once I was old enough to drive I started keeping count of how many times I was pulled over my first two years—fifteen. I also kept track of how many white officers were involved in my stops compared to black: twenty-seven out of thirty.

All in all, though, I count myself lucky in that I was never arrested. Because I never did anything for which I should have been arrested. A couple of fines for a broken taillight and not using my blinker signal when I made a left turn, but that was it.

*****

A lot of people, when they think about gangs in Los Angeles, picture them living and hanging out in high-rise edifices like the Robert Taylor Homes Project or the Cabrini-Green Housing Project, both of which are in Chicago.

Some gang members did live in projects, but they were more modest two- or three-story apartment buildings.

Others, like my friends who were gang members, lived in regular single-family houses, similar to Tre Styles's home in the 1991 movie, *Boyz n the Hood*. And my friends didn't hang out at projects; they hung out at "Blue" Billy's place.

My father and I lived across the street from "Blue" Billy Radditz's house in a comfortable two-story, two-bedroom bungalow, with a nice little front porch where the two of us sat on hot summer evenings and watched people as they strolled up and down the street.

Dad would sip his Old English 800 and smoke his Camels, which I constantly preached would be the death of him. I was hooked on Coke—the kind you drank, not the kind you put up your nose. We'd sit there and drink our drinks and munch on potato chips.

Across the street the Scarabs gathered out on Billy's front porch, drinking, smoking pot, laughing, bragging, and telling dirty jokes.

While our other neighbors—the non-gang type—always appeared to feel comfortable walking our block when my father was on our porch, I'm not sure I remember them ever doing so when he wasn't.

*****

As a kid, I was always shorter than all my friends. Consequently, though my favorite sport was basketball, I sucked at it. I couldn't even get the ball up to the rim until I was seven. I say rim, not basket, because none of our rims had nets.

By the time I turned nine, I could at least dribble the ball—sort of. And play the game—sort of. All summer long I would be outside, either at the park or the rec center, looking for somebody to play against, usually one on one. Sometimes I went to the alley behind Gilmore's Dairy where old man Gilmore had put up a rim—again, only a rim: no net—for us kids to use, on the supposition that after an hour or two of basketball we'd be so tired and hot and sweaty we'd go into the dairy and buy an ice cream cone or a milkshake.

Red Hot ice cream, made with red hot candy, was my favorite.

As I said, my favorite sport was basketball. And the decade of the eighties, at least as far as professional basketball was concerned, belonged to the Lakers.

In the twelve years from 1980—the year before I was born—to 1991 they appeared in the championship game nine times, winning five titles. Who was their star? The great Magic Johnson.

20

Whom I idolized.

As did every other kid I knew.

That's why our world was rocked that night in 1991 when Magic went on television and said he was retiring because he had HIV.

I knew what HIV was. In my neighborhood, every kid knew what HIV was and what it meant.

It meant you were a queer.

Magic Johnson: my hero—a queer. You might as well have told me my dad was a serial killer.

It shook my world.

And although my father took great pains to explain to me that Magic wasn't queer, that a heterosexual—yes, he had to explain to me what that meant, too—could get HIV just like a homosexual—I already knew what that meant—it was a couple more years before I believed it.

What I learned from that experience was that even heroes can make mistakes; no one is perfect.

*****

One day I was in the kitchen making a peanut butter and jelly sandwich when my father burst through the back door.

"Go to the bathroom and lock the door," he shouted. "And don't come out until I tell you to."

I froze, taken aback by the note of alarm in his voice.

"Quick, move!" he shouted again.

I jumped up, grabbed the boom box I'd received three days earlier for my eleventh birthday, and headed for the bathroom.

Dutifully, I locked the door, sat down on the floor, and switched on the radio, regretting that, in my haste, I had forgotten to take my sandwich.

I'd been aware of what had been the main topic in our neighborhood for the last few days: the trial of some white police officers for the beating of Rodney King a year earlier. Everyone knew who Rodney King was.

And everyone on my block—everyone in my neighborhood—had serious doubts about whether or not the officers would be found guilty. After all, there wasn't a single black person on the jury.

Still, there had been hope justice would prevail. At least, justice as *we* saw it.

But now, according to the announcer, the verdict was in: all four officers had been acquitted.

My father told me later it hadn't taken long for the rioting to begin. Four blocks from where we lived, the Pay-Less Liquor and Deli where my father bought his weekly bottle of Old English 800 was broken into. David Lee, the son of Samuel Lee, the owner, had been hurt, the plate glass door broken, and liquor taken. My father was one of two officers who responded, but by the time they arrived everyone was gone but the Lees.

I waited until I heard the front door close and I was sure my father had left. I wasn't content to listen to the radio. I figured there'd be something on television.

Cautiously, I opened the bathroom door and crept out. I checked all the rooms to make sure I was alone.

I grabbed my sandwich which still sat untouched on the kitchen counter and hurried to the living room. I switched on the TV and flopped onto the couch. For the next six hours, I sat and watched, entranced, while my neighborhood was looted and burned, praying the people doing the vandalizing would stay away from my street.

Around seven o'clock, I watched as a news helicopter broadcast a live feed of what was happening within a block from where Mr. Lee's store had been vandalized. A truck stopped at the traffic light and the driver—I could see he was white—was dragged out by a mob of men—all of them black—who began to hit and kick him. I recognized one of the men from the neighborhood, Damian Williams, when he threw a brick and hit the man in the head.

When the men tired of beating the man, they ran off, leaving him on the ground. I watched him struggle to get back into his cab as another black man approached him. I recognized the second man, too: Bobby Green, Jr. I was afraid the poor guy in the truck was going to get dragged out and beaten some more. But Bobby was talking to him and then he stepped up into the cab and the truck drove off.

When my father came in around ten, he looked as though *he'd* been beaten. Well, not literally. He just looked exhausted. He didn't even say anything about me not being in the bathroom.

"Go to bed," he said.

"You okay?" I asked.

"You been watching what's going on out there?"

I nodded.

"Hoodlums," he said. He looked at me, a stern expression on his grizzled face. "I better never find you've turned out like those turds. Come on, let's go to bed. I got to get up early tomorrow."

*****

There was no school the next day. The mayor had imposed a dusk to dawn curfew.

My father made it clear I was not to go outside. I assured him I had no intention of leaving the house.

23

He left for work and I turned the TV on: more coverage of the rioting that had now expanded from my neighborhood northward.

I watched, spellbound, as live coverage showed some Korean shopkeepers armed with handguns, M1 carbines, Ruger Mini-14s, and pump-action shotguns, exchanging gunfire with armed looters.

Even though I was black, I found myself rooting for the Koreans.

About two o'clock, another of my friends, Winston, knocked on the front door. Winston was older than me, almost fifteen.

"What are you doing here?" I asked as I let him in. "You should be home. It's dangerous out there."

"That's why I have this," he said. He pulled a gun from his coat pocket.

I jumped back.

"Where'd you get that?" I whispered, as if my father, not even in the house, might hear.

"Ain't she a beauty?" said Winston. His eyes gleamed as he waved the gun over his head. "It's a Glock 17."

"Where'd you get it?" I asked again. "Did you buy it?"

Winston snickered. "Buy it? Fuck, no, I didn't *buy* it. I fucking *stole* it."

"You stole it?"

"Yeah, me and some of the guys broke into that pawnshop over on the boulevard; picked it up there."

I stared at the gun. "What are you going to do with it?"

"Do with it? I'm going to fucking shoot any mother-fucker who tries to shoot me. Or tries to stab me, or throws something at me. I hope somebody fucking tries."

"You've got to go," I said, hustling him to the front door. "If my dad comes in and finds you with that, he'll arrest you."

Winston stood in the doorway, scowling at me. "And I'll fucking shoot him if he tries," he said. Then he turned and walked out onto the porch and down the steps.

That evening someone—the person was never caught—shot and killed Winston.

Three days later the mayor lifted the curfew and the city, including our neighborhood, returned to comparative normalcy.

CHAPTER FOUR
(thirty-six days until the Presidential election)

Other than for business meetings, Bobby eschewed going out for lunch. Instead, as they were doing this day, he and Kevin ate in Bobby's office where the normal topic of discussion was the University of California, Santa Barbara sports teams.

Twenty-five years ago Kevin Sperling had been a freshman at the school. A black kid from the Watts area of Los Angeles, he was working his way through college with the help of his mother, who toiled fourteen hours a day cleaning houses in the exclusive community of Brentwood, riding a bus roundtrip every day but Sunday, her one day off. His father had walked out when Kevin was three.

He'd met Bobby Winslow their first day on campus. They'd become fast friends, rooming together their freshman year in a dorm, later in an apartment in Isla Vista for their final three years.

Bobby took a bite of his sandwich.

"Tuna salad again?" said Kevin. "Don't you ever eat anything else for lunch?"

Bobby's favorite lunch was tuna. Kevin couldn't stand it.

"Why don't you like it," Bobby had asked the first time the subject came up.

"That seems like all we ever had at home when I was growing up," Kevin answered. "We couldn't afford anything else. I got sick and tired of the damn stuff."

Bobby looked at the sandwich in his hand. "I *like* tuna salad. Ku fixes my lunch for me. Besides, it's not tuna salad. This is something different; it's chuna salad. It's the one thing he knows how to make."

Kevin's brow furrowed. "*Chuna* salad?"

"Two-thirds tuna, one-third chicken, hard-boiled eggs, mayonnaise, and Grey Poupon."

Kevin's nose wrinkled in disgust. "There is such a thing as lunch meat. And you could fix your own lunch, you know."

"Kevin, I'm the Governor of California. I shouldn't *have* to fix my own lunch."

Kevin shook his head and took a bite of his sandwich.

"What'd your wife fix you?" asked Bobby.

Kevin blushed. "Peanut butter and jelly—same as she fixed the kids."

"Don't say another word about my chuna salad," said Bobby, laughing

Kevin decided to change the subject.

"On another note—this is a real fucking mess, you know? With McClaren dropping dead."

Bobby started to respond when his phone buzzed. He pushed a button and Jeanette's voice came over the intercom.

"Sir, I know you didn't want to be disturbed, but I have Congressman Gilley on the line."

"The head of the national committee?" asked Bobby, surprised.

"Yes, sir."

"Which line?"

"Three."

Bobby pushed another button. "Thornton?"

"Hey, Bobby," came Thornton's voice over the speaker.

"God, you gotta be pulling your hair out about now," said Bobby.

Thornton Gilley sat at his desk, tapping it with a pencil. He raised his hand and rubbed it over his head, bald as a hard-boiled egg, and chuckled. "I would be if I had any."

"Well," said Bobby, "as Oliver Hardy would say, 'Stan, this is a fine mess you've gotten us into this time.'"

"Tell me about it. Things are going crazy right now. Listen, I need to talk with you."

"Okay."

"Not now. And not over the phone."

"Where are you?"

"D.C. I'm flying into Sacramento tonight. Can I meet you at your home about eight?"

"Sure. See you then." Bobby pushed another button, ending the call. He looked at Kevin. "He wants to meet with me."

"What do you think he wants?"

"Unless Forrester's willing to take on the job, I have a feeling the committee's thinking about asking Josh Green to take McClaren's place."

"Forrester? The V.P. candidate? Isn't he like . . . in his seventies?"

Bobby nodded.

"And Green? Isn't he running again for the Senate?"

"Yeah, but if he has a chance to run for President I think he'd take it. Thornton knows I know Josh from when I served with him in the Senate. I bet he wants to pick my brain to see what I think about him as a candidate."

"What *do* you think?"

"I think he'd make a hell of a president. He's served two terms. I'd bet he's ready to move on."

"I sure hope they find somebody who can beat your dad. Is it true he thinks Dubya was the greatest president ever?"

"That is definitely not true. Dubya's only second on his list."

"No way! Who's first?"

"Dick Cheney," said Bobby, grinning.

Jeanette heard the laughter even from her office.

CHAPTER FIVE

Alice O'Shea still lived in the two-bedroom house she and her now long-dead husband, Darren, occupied when the latter was killed eighteen years earlier, a murder that had never been solved.

The two thousand dollars she'd been receiving at the time of Darren's death from an undisclosed source had come to an end. The minuscule amount of social security benefits she received from Darren's employment plus welfare and a small disability payment were scarcely enough to pay the rent and keep her in food, medicine, beer, and cigarettes.

She'd tried taking in ironing but found standing on her feet all day too much for her.

Lately, she hadn't felt well. Although well was a relative term. She hadn't felt well for a long time. Now she felt even worse.

She flipped on the TV and had just laid down on the couch to watch it when she heard the kitchen door open.

"Shit," she murmured, the thought crossing her mind that she failed to lock the door. This wasn't the kind of neighborhood where you wanted to forget something like that.

Warily, she got to her feet. Then she heard P.J.'s voice call out.

"Alice?"

Alice breathed a sigh of relief.

"Coming," she said.

When she reached the kitchen P.J. was hanging up her coat.

"Honey!" said Alice, beaming. "I was wondering if you'd be by."

P.J. kissed Alice on the cheek. She noticed she was still in her robe, though it was three o'clock in the afternoon.

"You want a beer?" asked Alice.

"Always," said P.J.

Moments later they sat at the kitchen table, puffing away on Lucky Strikes, a bottle of Budweiser in front of each of them.

"It's been a while. I wanted to see how you were doing," said P.J. She reached over and took Alice's hand.

"I guess as good as can be expected," said Alice. She started to cough.

P.J. jumped up and hurried to the sink to get a glass of water.

"Here," she said when she returned to the table. She handed the glass to Alice. "Drink this."

Alice took a few sips, then handed the glass back.

"More," said P.J., authoritatively.

Alice drank a little more and set the glass down. "I'm okay now. I got an appointment with the doctor Thursday. Try to find out what this damn cough's all about. So, where's our boy?"

"I dropped him off at the mosque for his prayer time."

Alice shook her head. "I still don't understand why he wanted to become an A-rab; and changing his name to Momad, or Moomad, or whatever."

"Muhammad. And not an Arab—a Muslim. And I don't understand it either, but it's important to him."

"Arab, Muslim. It's all the same to me. How's the band doing?"

"Great! They've got about a dozen gigs lined up around the District. Making enough to pay the rent and keep me in beer and cigarettes."

Alice raised her bottle of beer. "Here's to beer and cigarettes."

They clinked their bottles together and each took another swig.

"How's your job going?" asked Alice.

"I have something in the fire that's going to take some research. And, frankly, I'm not sure where to begin."

"Can you tell me about it?"

"Not yet—too early. But if it works out it could be really big. I'm concerned about that cough. You've had it way too long."

"I'll find out Thursday. Probably ain't nothing. Let's have another beer."

QUINCY'S STORY - CHAPTER II

When my father was three years old his family moved from Georgia to New York City. That's where he grew up and lived until he joined the army when he was eighteen. He was a lifelong Knicks fan, especially of their star player, Patrick Ewing.

In 1994, the Knicks, playing against the Houston Rockets, were in the finals for the first time since 1973, when they'd won the championship.

My father and I were watching game five on KNBC when it was interrupted by the coverage of police cars chasing what turned out to be a white Ford Bronco in which O. J. Simpson was riding.

"Crap!" cried my father. "Where's the game? What happened to the game?"

But within minutes he and I were both engrossed in the scene playing out on our TV. For the next hour, like millions of other viewers across the nation, we watched, mesmerized by the spectacle unfolding right out there in our own neighborhood.

After the chase ended, the TV station put up a split screen that showed both events, the car chase and the end of the game.

My father was ecstatic when the Knicks won, 91-84.

I was getting ready for bed when a friend of my father's, Mr. Watkins, dropped by.

I listened from my bedroom as he and my father discussed, not the game, but the situation surrounding O. J.

Mr. Watkins took a sip of the beer my father had handed him, then asked, "What do you think? Did he kill them?"

"Crap, no," my father responded. "He's being set up for this."

"I agree," said Mr. Watkins. "The whiteys are looking to find him guilty 'cause he's a big star."

"Damn right," said my father.

They continued discussing the situation.

I fell asleep listening to them.

When I woke the next morning I had come to my own conclusion: my father and Mr. Watkins were right—O. J. *was* being set up.

Once again a black man was getting hosed by the system.

We were all—we, being the black community—overjoyed when, a year later, O. J. was found not guilty.

We were not as happy when a year and a half after that he was found guilty in a wrongful death suit.

CHAPTER SIX
(thirty-six days until the Presidential election)

Nate Jackson was not one of Jamie's favorite people. Eighteen months earlier Robert had fired his former Chief of Staff, Norman Kunzman, a lifetime friend, and replaced him with Jackson.

At the same time, Jackson had little love for Jamie: he felt the President's aide was not someone to be trusted.

Nate sat in a chair in Robert's suite while Jamie stretched out on the couch. Robert spoke into the phone, as he ate his lunch.

"Elizabeth, Mrs. Winslow and I both want you to know how sorry we were to hear of Jerry's untimely passing. I know it must have been a great shock to you."

Robert speared a sausage patty with his fork and stuffed it into his mouth, chewing while he listened to McClaren's widow's response.

"He was a formidable opponent," said Robert. "It would have been one hell of an election."

Robert motioned for Jamie to bring him a newspaper from a table across the room.

Jamie jumped up, grabbed the paper, hurried to Robert's side, and handed it to him.

Robert laid the fork down and began to scan the front page.

"That's right," he said, as he continued to read. "Now, Elizabeth, if there's anything either Wilma or I or any of my staff can do for you, you be sure and let us know, okay?"

Robert rolled his eyes.

"Right. You, too. Take care now.

"I swear," said Robert, hanging up the phone, "that woman can talk the ears off a cornstalk. Okay, here's the first thing we do. Whatever I have scheduled the rest of the week, cancel it. And tell Ivan to cut back on the campaign."

"You think that's wise?" asked Nate. "I mean, the Democrats will find *somebody* to fill the ticket."

Robert looked at Nate, his fork halfway to his mouth. "Like who? That old fart, Forrester? Shit, I hope he does run. I'll never have to make another campaign speech again."

Nate shook his head. "The word I've heard is he's not interested—didn't even want to run for Vice-President. My sources tell me they're looking at someone off the radar, that Gilley already has someone in mind."

"Who?" asked Robert and Jamie in unison.

"Don't know," said Nate.

"Find out," said Robert. "I'd like to know before I have to read it in the fucking newspaper."

"Yes, sir. Is there anything else?"

"Cancel the Seattle trip. Let's get back to Washington. I didn't want to have to talk to a bunch of fucking niggers anyway."

CHAPTER SEVEN

Thornton Gilley, distinguished-looking, in his early seventies, dressed in a sports jacket and slacks, sat in a beach chair beside the pool of the California Governor's mansion. Bobby, more casually dressed in shorts, a golf shirt, and barefoot, stood at the wet bar. Ku'ualoha lounged nearby, playing with Kula, his and Bobby's Golden Retriever, named after the area on Maui where Ku'ualoha grew up.

"Drink?" Bobby asked Gilley.

"Please. I can use one."

"Scotch as I recall," said Bobby.

Gilley nodded.

"Ku, you want a drink?" Bobby called out.

"No, thanks," Ku'ualoha answered.

Bobby poured two drinks, walked over to Gilley, handed him a glass, then sat down in the other beach chair.

"So, what's on your mind?" he asked. "As if I didn't know."

"You're right," said Gilley. "This *is* a hell of a mess we're in."

"What about Forrester? Is he ready to step up?"

"Huh, uh. He didn't want to be on the ticket in the first place. Only reason he agreed to was because he knew we needed him to carry Ohio. And if Jerry did win, Tom only planned to serve one term. He never expected Jerry to die in office, let alone before he ever got there."

"What now?"

"You know what will happen if your dad gets another term?" asked Gilley.

"You mean, besides the country going to hell in a handbasket?"

Gilley laughed. "Yes, that and more. There's a good chance he'd get a shot at shifting the Supreme Court even further to the right."

"What do you mean?"

"Emerson and Hornagle are both in ill health. Word is, they've been holding on until we get a Democrat back in the White House before they retire . . . or kick the bucket, whichever comes first."

"You're right," said Bobby. "If those two go while my father's in office, he'll for sure pick two more conservatives."

"That's not all. Even if either one of them should continue on the court, my sources say your father might try to take a play out of FDR's playbook."

"How's that?"

"In 1937, when Roosevelt was working to get his New Deal programs in place, he tried to convince Congress to pass legislation to allow up to fifteen justices."

"Is that legal?"

"It's legal alright. The legislation would have allowed him to appoint an additional justice for any current one over seventy who wouldn't retire."

"But it didn't happen," said Bobby.

"No. Congress didn't go along with it."

"How about this one?"

"I don't think so, since we have the Senate, but I wouldn't bet on it, either. In any event, we have to come up with a replacement for McClaren, one who can beat your dad."

"How about one of the other guys who ran against Jerry?"

"No," said Gilley. "None of them got more than five percent of the votes. Jerry was a runaway winner."

"So you're thinking about Josh Green?"

Gilley looked surprised. "Josh? No." He picked up his glass and took a deep drink.

"We're thinking about you."

Bobby's drink stopped halfway to his lips.

"Me? You're thinking about *me*? You've got to be kidding!"

"I am dead serious. I met with the committee by phone this morning and you're the one we want."

"Okay, first of all, you know I'm gay."

Gilley shook his head. "We don't think that'll make any difference. We've sent an African-American to the White House and almost sent a woman."

"*Should* have sent a woman," said Bobby.

"Yes, well the thing is—the country's ready for a gay president."

"*Ready* for a gay president?"

Gilley chuckled. "Okay, maybe not *ready*. *Needs* might be a better word."

"But . . . why me?"

"You're hot right now. The keynote address you gave at the convention put you in the national spotlight, just like Obama's did in '04. As the Governor of California, you can carry the state. And, there's one more thing."

"And that is?"

"You're his son. There are a lot of people in this country who would vote for your father even though they don't like him. Given a good enough excuse, they'll vote against him. *You're* that good excuse. They'd love to see you kick his butt. Okay, and I guess there's one more thing than the last thing: we all think you'd make a terrific president."

"Man, I don't know," said Bobby. "I was never sure I wanted to be a governor. Now you want me to run for *President?*"

He gulped down his drink. "You need an answer right now?"

"If you can give it; otherwise, I'll need to know no later than noon tomorrow. We're playing catch-up right now. We have to get a new campaign underway. You know Hank Snow?"

Bobby nodded.

"He was McClaren's campaign manager. We'd prefer to keep him on, whoever the new candidate is. But that's not necessarily set in stone, depending upon what the next guy wants. We have to make sure all the voting machines get reprogrammed with the new candidate's name. It'll take a hell of a lot of work. Plus, the debate in Washington is scheduled for four weeks from tonight."

"You're not going to cancel it?" asked Bobby.

"Not a chance. It's our best shot at negating whatever kind of bump your dad's going to get from McClaren's death. Look, I have a red-eye back to D.C. tonight. Call me at my office in the morning. Or, better yet, here, call me on my cell phone."

Gilley took out a business card, wrote a number on the back, and handed the card to Bobby.

"Bobby, we're counting on you."

Bobby took the card and studied it. "I'll let you know. I gotta tell you, right now I don't see it happening. But I'll talk it over with Ku—get his input."

"Sure," said Gilley.

Though he had been occupied playing with the dog, Ku'ualoha had overheard every word of the conversation. As soon as Gilley left the pool area and disappeared inside the house, he walked over and sat down next to Bobby.

"You seriously thinking about this?" he asked.

Bobby shrugged. "Not seriously. But I do have to give it some consideration."

"I think it's a fantastic idea."

"You do?" said Bobby.

"Sure. That would make me the first gentleman, wouldn't it?"

"I guess . . . if we were married."

"I couldn't be called your mistress. That doesn't fit at all."

"I think there's an Italian term for a man who is the lover of a married woman, but it doesn't fit either."

"What's the term?" asked Ku.

"Cavalier Servente."

"Ooh," said Ku'ualoha. "That's cool! That's what we'll call me when you're the number one man."

"Yeah, let's talk about it tomorrow over breakfast. I'm beat. This has been one hell of a day."

CHAPTER EIGHT
(thirty-five days until the Presidential election)

Bobby looked at the dish on the breakfast table. "Loco moco?" he asked

"Good morning, Sunshine."

Ku'ualoha's greeting was bright, almost giddy. "Yes, loco moco."

Loco moco was Bobby's favorite Hawaiian dish: white rice, topped with a fried egg, hamburger patty, and brown gravy, to which Ku'ualoha had added linguica and shrimp.

"What's the occasion?" asked Bobby.

"Because today I have the feeling you're going to be named the new presidential candidate for the Democratic Party, which would make me the Cavalier Servente, and I thought we should start the day off right with a good breakfast."

"I didn't think you knew how to make anything but chuna salad."

"I have many hidden talents. Sit down. Let's eat and discuss our future."

*****

Flying on Air Force One with the President and his entourage was a new experience for Clay Lincoln. They had left St. Louis and were on their way to the District. Bob Lindsey, who normally reported for the San Diego Times, had taken ill and Clay had filled in at the last minute. He sat with a dozen other reporters as Robert held a press conference.

He wasn't sure what impressed him more: the deep, leather lounge seats assigned to each reporter or the well-stocked, open bar.

Jamie, along with Ivan Sivinski, Robert's campaign manager, and Oren Masterson, who handled polling for the campaign, stood lined up against the rear wall.

"No, I haven't the foggiest notion if the team will ever win another Super Bowl," said Robert, in response to a question. "Maybe all those people who want them to actually have a name for the team are right: maybe they'd win if they were—oh, I don't know—the Washington Wonderkinds?"

Polite laughter filled the room.

Robert acknowledged the raised hand of one of the reporters.

"Bill, you have a question?"

Bill Jensen stood. "Mr. President, what's happening with the conflict in Guinea? Are we making any progress in eliminating the terrorist militias operating there?"

Robert's face tightened.

"Bill, I'm glad you asked that question. When we sent armed troops into Guinea I publicly vowed we wouldn't leave until every Muslim—I mean every terrorist"—Robert hastily corrected himself—"was killed or captured. We have made great strides since then and have taken back two-thirds of the country."

"But at such a high price in terms of civilians killed," said Jensen.

"There are collateral damages in any military operation," said Robert. "That cannot be avoided."

Jensen started to speak again, but Robert saw Ivan at the rear of the room hold up one finger.

"Thank you for giving me the finger, Ivan," said Robert, eliciting another round of laughter. "Okay, one more question."

Jensen sat down as a number of hands shot up, including that of Kelly Fitzgerald who was sitting in the front row. Attractive, in her twenties with flaming red hair, Kelly wore a dress that did little to conceal her more than adequate figure. Showing a tad more cleavage than appropriate, the dress was more than a little immodest for a presidential press conference.

Robert seemed not to notice. "Kelly," he said.

"Mr. President, your dog—Templar, is it? I notice he doesn't travel with you. I wondered why that is and how you came up with his name."

"Unfortunately, Templar gets airsick," said Robert, smiling.

Again, laughter filled the room.

"And Templar was named to honor the Knights Templars who fought in the Crusades."

"The Crusades?" said Kelly. "The Holy Wars fought by Christians against the Muslims?"

"That's right. Although at that time they were known as Mohammedans, or Saracens, or Moslems. Thank all of you for the opportunity of answering your questions. Enjoy the refreshments."

Everyone stood and began shuffling toward the door. Robert motioned Jamie to him and whispered something in his ear. Jamie hurried to the door in time to catch Kelly before she left.

"Miss Fitzgerald," said Jamie. "The President wondered if you might stay behind for a moment. He has something he wants to give you."

"Of course," said Kelly.

Jamie waited until the last reporter exited, then left and closed the door behind him, leaving Robert and Kelly alone in the room.

Most of the reporters who emptied out of the briefing room had moved to the press seating section of the plane, and were engaged in various tasks: typing, writing notes, listening to recorders via earphones.

Seated next to Harry Anderson, White House Correspondent for the Washington Eagle, Clay finished filing his report and slammed his laptop closed.

"I hate this goddamn thing!" he said.

Harry looked at him. "Don't let the president hear you saying that."

"What do you mean?"

"Taking the Lord's name in vain."

"Are you kidding me?" said Clay. "I've heard him say a lot worse."

"Oh, he swears alright—like a trooper. But he never says . . ." Harry leaned over and whispered, ". . . goddamn or Jesus Christ or even Jesus." He straightened back up. "And if he hears you saying it, you might get drawn and quartered and tossed out of the plane, never mind we're thirty thousand feet up."

"Is he that religious?"

"Depends. In some areas, yes. In others . . . let's just say his Christian faith has holes in it."

"Like what?"

Harry looked around, then back at Clay. He spoke in a low voice. "Like he's a racist son-of-a-bitch for one thing. He hates gays, Muslims, Jews, and anybody whose skin color is other than white."

"What do gays have to do with racism? And he has African-Americans and Hispanics in his administration."

"Gays because of his son, I suppose. And—correction: he has one of each, an African-American and an Hispanic—his token minority members; wouldn't look good if the whole group was lily-white. He also has a thing for the ladies."

"What do you mean?"

"Like getting into their pants every chance he gets."

"Come on! I don't believe that!"

"Yeah, ask the redhead back there. I bet she's been down that road a few times."

Clay swiveled around and looked, then turned back to Harry.

"Which one is she?"

Harry glanced over his shoulder. "Huh. I don't see her. Wonder where she disappeared to."

He turned back, reached over, and shook Clay's hand. "Harry Anderson, Washington Eagle."

"Clay. Clay Lincoln—San Diego Times."

"What happened to Bob?"

"Got a bug or something. I'm filling in for him."

"First time aboard?"

"Yeah," said Clay. "It's something, isn't it?"

"Sure is. And we don't get to see half of it."

"What was all that about the Crusades?"

"Oh, he's an authority on them," said Harry. "I hear he's read every book ever written about them. Knows the dates and leaders of each one, and what happened."

"And the Templars?"

"You know how for some guys their heroes are athletes or politicians or entertainers? His are the Knights Templar. He was in DeMolay when he was younger. In fact, when he was elected president he was also elected to the DeMolay Hall of Fame. I guess you could say the Crusades are an obsession with him."

"I guess it stands to reason if he hates Muslims like you say he does."

"He lost a cousin in the Twin Towers. I heard they were as close as brothers. Believe me, I bet if Robert Winslow could wave a magic wand and make every Muslim disappear off the face of the earth, he would."

*****

Jamie was leaning against the Press Briefing Room door reading a newspaper when Nate approached.

"Is he in there?" asked Nate.

"He's kind of busy right now," said Jamie, without looking up from his paper.

"This is important."

"I really don't think you want to disturb him."

"Get out of my way."

Nate grabbed Jamie by the arm and moved him away from the door. He turned the handle: locked.

"Mr. President, it's Nate. I have to speak to you. It's extremely important."

Nate heard Robert's voice from the other side of the door.

"Hold on. I'm coming."

Inside the briefing room, Kelly was bent forward over a chair, her dress up over her back, while Robert stood behind her, his pants down around his ankles. A light sweat covered his face. Kelly moaned as silently as she could while Robert continued to pump her.

He thrust more rapidly, grunted, then relaxed.

Moments later the press room door opened revealing Kelly, looking somewhat disheveled. Robert stood behind her, adjusting his tie.

Kelly turned to Robert and smiled. "Thank you, Mr. President."

"Anytime, Miss Fitzgerald," said Robert. "It was my pleasure."

Passing through the doorway, Kelly continued down the corridor. The three men watched her as she went.

"What is it?" asked Robert, after she disappeared into the press seating section.

"There's been a development," said Nate.

Robert motioned Nate into the briefing room and closed the door. Jamie moved closer in an attempt to hear what was being said, but with little success.

Moments later, Robert's agitated voice could be heard loud and clear.

"Are you fucking shitting me?"

Inside the room, Robert jumped up from where he'd been leaning back against a chair, his face livid.

"No, sir," said Nate. "I confirmed it. Your son is the new Democratic candidate."

"That little shit! You know he's doing this just to piss me off. Well, let him try. Has Ivan done anything yet about dialing back the campaign?"

"No, sir."

Robert began to pace the room. "Good. In fact, I want to bump it up: more TV ads, more internet ads, more of that twitter shit. I don't care how much it costs. Call Ivan right now and tell him."

Robert pounded the podium with his fist.

"I'm going to bury that little fucker so deep he'll be lucky if he ever gets elected to any office again."

48

"Yes, sir."

"Tell Jamie to come in here."

Nate left and in a few moments, Jamie appeared.

"I want to see Madeline tonight," said Robert.

"Um, are you sure . . . ?"

"Just do it."

CHAPTER NINE

Lilly Adkins, Wilma's personal secretary, cuddled a tan and white Chihuahua in her arms as she watched the Presidential helicopter gently set down.

Once the VH-72P "Eagle's" blades stopped rotating, Robert, Wilma, Nate, Jamie, and Oren disembarked and headed toward the White House.

Lilly set the dog down and it took off on a beeline for Robert, who gathered it up in his arms and nuzzled it.

"Hey, Templar, did you miss me?" said Robert, as he continued toward the building. Lilly set off in a different direction.

The group entered through a door flanked by two Marines who saluted when Robert passed by. Inside, men in suits and several more Marines waited in the corridor.

"Welcome back, sir," said one of the men, Evan Standard.

Robert nodded and continued on.

Evan leaned into the man next to him and whispered something.

Robert stopped. He turned and walked back to Evan.

"Did you say something?" asked Robert, locking Evan's eyes with his.

"Uh, no, sir, Mr. President," mumbled Evan.

"I'm pretty sure you did," said Robert. He looked at the man to whom Evan had spoken. "Did you hear what he said?"

"Uh, yes, sir, I did."

"Would you care to tell me what he said?"

"Uh, no, sir, I'd rather not."

"I want to hear it," said Robert. "I'd like to know if I heard what I thought I heard."

"Uh, sir, I believe he said she looked like she'd been ridden hard and put away wet."

"Then I guess I did hear what I thought I heard." Robert looked at Evan. "What's your name, son?"

"E . . . Evan, sir. Evan Standard."

"Can I assume you were referring to Mrs. Winslow since she's the only female present?"

Evan stammered. "I . . . uh, y . . . yes, sir. I was."

"Do you agree you owe Mrs. Winslow an apology?" asked Robert.

"Yes, sir, I do."

Evan didn't say anything.

"And?" said Robert, the tone of his voice clear he was becoming angrier.

Evan jerked. "Uh, Mrs. Winslow, I apologize for what I said. It was stupid of me."

Wilma nodded. "Thank you."

"What's your job, Evan?" asked Robert.

"I work in data entry, Mr. President."

"Is it a good job?"

"Yes, sir, it is. Best job I've ever had."

"'Had' is the right word there. Evan, you're fired."

Evan was dumbfounded. "Sir?"

"Fired," said Robert, "in that, I want your ass out of here."

"Dear, I don't—" Wilma started to say.

"I'll handle this," said Robert. He turned to one of the Marines. "Corporal, please escort Mr. Standard to his desk or his locker or wherever it is he keeps his personal effects. Once he has secured those, escort him to the main gate and inform security to recover his pass and any other form of identification he could use to allow himself access to the White House."

"Yes, sir."

"I don't ever want to see your face again, understand?" Robert said to Evan.

"Yes, sir," said Evan, trying without much success to stop his shaking.

Robert turned and resumed his walk down the corridor, the entourage following behind.

Wilma took Robert's hand. "Thank you, dear."

"The wife of the President of the United States deserves respect," said Robert, "if for no other reason than her position."

Robert removed his hand from Wilma's and continued walking.

"Besides, what that man said about you was disrespectful of me."

Wilma looked at Robert. She had a sad expression on her face.

QUINCY'S STORY - CHAPTER III

As I look back now, 1999 was definitely the worst year of my life.

It started off with a big disappointment. I'd been crushed when my favorite college football team, the UCLA Bruins, were upset the previous month by Miami and, as a consequence, were going to miss out on playing in the first BCS Championship game. Until then, the team was ranked number two in the country and appeared a cinch to meet number one Tennessee.

Instead, the Bruins were now set to face off against Wisconsin and their star running back, Ron Dayne, in the Rose Bowl.

Okay, the Rose Bowl wasn't chopped liver. But it wasn't for the championship, either.

My best friend, Richie Baumgardner—by now, all my earlier childhood friends were dead—had invited me and about a half dozen of his other friends over to his house to watch the game on TV. Since my father was on duty that day, it seemed like a good idea, instead of staying home and watching it by myself.

Richie, a senior in high school like me, lived in a nice home in a different part of town from where I lived; a much nicer part of town. His father was a lawyer and his mother worked in a travel agency. I knew his sister, Penelope, some three years younger than the two of us, had a crush on me because Richie told me so.

Richie's family had money and they loved to spend it.

We were watching the game on their forty-two-inch flat-screen TV, groaning when Dayne spun off a fifty-four-yard run for a touchdown, then cheering when our own star, Cade McNown, connected with Jermaine Lewis on a thirty-eight-yard pass to tie the score.

When the quarter ended, Richie left to get each of us a beer. I heard the doorbell ring.

"Hey, Cue, get that, will you?" Richie called out from the kitchen.

When I opened the door, I was struck by the sight of the gorgeous girl who stood in front of me. Although I was only five-foot-nine, I towered over her by a good six or seven inches. Her hair was hidden by some sort of a scarf—I found out later it was called a hijab—but a face the color of creamy coffee peeked out from under it, a face whose main attraction was a pair of dark, deep-set eyes that almost seemed to be swimming.

Or possibly it was only my head that was swimming.

A man taller than me stood behind her.

"Hi," the tall man said. "I'm Faizan. Richie invited us over to watch the game."

I nodded, too overcome by how beautiful the girl was to say anything.

After a few seconds passed with me not moving and looking, I'm sure, like a lost fawn, Faizan spoke again. "Okay if we come in?"

"Oh . . . oh, sure. I'm sorry," I mumbled, as I moved aside to let them pass by.

Richie returned from the kitchen just as we all entered the living room.

"Faizan. Where've you been?" asked Richie. "You missed the first quarter."

"Prayers," said Faizan, as he settled into an easy chair. The girl found a place on the sofa.

The other guys in the room were too busy replaying the game to pay any attention to the new arrivals.

"Oh, right," said Richie, handing me a beer. "I forgot. Anyway, glad you could make it. You want a soda?" he asked, looking first to Faizan, then to the girl. "Memona?"

Memona? That was her name?

Memona shook her head. "No, thanks."

Her voice was lilting, as lovely as she was.

I headed for the sofa and sat down next to her, leaving the other end for Richie.

"So you're Memona?" I said.

"I am," she said. "And you are . . . ?"

"Oh, sorry. Quincy. Quincy Bollweber."

A little grin spread over her face.

"I know," I said. "It's a strange name. My friends call me Cue."

"No stranger than mine," said Memona.

"Memona's not so strange," I said, thinking it very much was.

"Sure it is. So's my last name: Farooqi."

"Okay," I said. "You're right—that *is* strange. What kind of a name is it?"

"Pakistani. My family is from Pakistan."

"You sure speak good English," I said.

Hell, better than mine.

"I studied it in Pakistan before we came here," said Memona.

"And so you're Faizan's . . .?"

"Sister," replied Memona.

Thank God—not his girlfriend! I thought.

For the next half hour, I peppered Memona with questions, in the process discovering she and Faizan were Muslim and she attended a private school on the north side of town. She was seventeen, the same age as me. Her father was an orthopedic surgeon at a large hospital and her mother an accomplished author. She had two other brothers, both younger than her and Faizan.

I was about to ask her what she was studying in school when Richie spoke up.

"Okay, who wants some snacks?"

I looked at him. "Is the game over?" I asked.

"No, Cue, it's not over. It's halftime."

"Who's ahead?" I asked. I glanced at the TV.

"Wisconsin by three. So . . ." Richie looked at Memona. "Memona? How about a soda now?"

"I'd love one," she responded.

I jumped up. "I'll get it," I said.

Richie followed me into the kitchen. When we got there he grabbed my arm and jerked me around. "What are you doing?" he asked.

I squinted, and my brow furrowed. "What? What do you mean?"

"What are you doing with Memona?"

"I think she's cute. No, more than cute—she's hot."

"She's Muslim. Her father wouldn't let you within a mile of her."

"Because I'm black?"

"No, stupid, because you're not a Muslim. I know. I made a play once and Faizan made it clear to me his father wasn't about to let her date a non-Muslim. I'd back off if I was you."

I felt my body stiffen. I stared at Richie.

"Yeah, but you're not me, are you?" I said.

"Hmph," Rickie snorted. "No, I'm not. And I have a feeling I'll be glad I'm not if you get involved with that girl."

We fixed the drinks and returned to the living room.

By the time the game finished and Memona left with Faizan, I'd talked her into giving me her phone number. At first, I was surprised when she said it was her cell phone number—*I* sure as hell couldn't afford a cell phone—but then I realized her family was probably as loaded as Richie's.

*****

The day after the Rose Bowl was a Saturday, so I knew Memona wouldn't be in school.

I wanted to call her as soon as I got up at eight but managed to restrain myself until eleven o'clock rolled around.

"Hey, it's Cue," I said when she answered the phone.

"Who?" came back the response from the other end of the line.

"Cue . . . Quincy. We met yesterday at Richie's."

"Oh, right. Hi." It was that same gentle voice that had enthralled me yesterday until the game was over and her brother said they had to go home for evening prayer.

"I was wondering . . . what are you up to today?"

"Nothing special. Hanging around the house."

"You want to get a bite to eat or something?"

After what seemed forever, Memona replied, "My . . . my father doesn't like for me to see . . ."

"Non-Muslims?" I said. "Yeah, Richie told me. But there are black Muslims. Muhammad Ali—he's a Muslim."

"Who's Muhammad Ali?"

"Who's Muhammad Ali? Are you kidding? Only the greatest boxer ever, that's who!"

"Sorry, I don't know him. So, are *you* Muslim?"

I hesitated before answering. "No, not really."

"Not really? What does that mean?"

I almost sensed the smile hiding behind her face.

"It means I could be—for the right reason."

"For the right reason?"

"Yeah, for the right reason."

"Do you know anything about Islam?" asked Memona.

"I know you worship Muhammad."

"Is that all you know?"

"I know you pray a lot," I said.

Memona laughed. "That's true—we do pray a lot. But we do not worship Muhammad—we worship Allah."

"Then who's Muhammad?"

After another brief pause, Memona said, "I could tell you more about my faith. That is, if you're interested."

"Yeah, yeah, that would be great!" I said. Anything to spend some time with her.

"Meet me at the library at two o'clock," said Memona.

"The library? Okay. Which one?"

"Vernon—on South Central."

*****

At twenty 'til two, I was waiting outside the door of the library.

At two-fifteen I was still there, wondering if Memona had blown me off. Then I saw her.

And once again I was struck by how utterly gorgeous she was.

She waved when she saw me. I waved back.

"I'm sorry I'm late," she said when she reached me. "I hope you didn't think I wasn't coming."

"Never crossed my mind," I lied.

Inside the library, we found a quiet corner with a small table and two chairs. She sat down first and pulled two books from her book bag. I sat down next to her.

The soft fragrance of her perfume drifted over me. It was subtle, hardly noticeable. I found out later wearing perfume in public was okay as long as it wasn't so strong it might be enticing to a man.

I have to admit even this faint scent was damned enticing to me.

"I brought two books for you to borrow," said Memona.

She picked up the first one. "This is the Qur'an. It is to us what your Bible is to you. I assume you are a Christian, are you not?"

I scrunched up my mouth. The only time I ever went to church was for funerals, of which I had attended too many in my relatively short life.

"I don't attend church," I said. "But I believe in God."

"That is good;" said Memona, "that you believe in God. Not so good you do not go to church."

She handed me the Qur'an.

"We Muslims believe the Qur'an to be the book of divine guidance revealed from Allah to Muhammad through the angel Gabriel. It is Allah's final revelation to humanity."

"Revelation?"

"It tells us how we should live our lives," said Memona.

"You believe in Allah, rather than God?" I asked.

"Some believe he is one and the same. You call Him God; we call Him Allah."

"*Some* do?"

"More strict Muslims do not, because you also believe your Jesus is God. We believe he is a prophet, like many others."

I nodded. "Okay. What's the other book?"

"*This is Muslims: Their Religious Beliefs and Practices.* It came out a few years ago. You might find it helpful."

For the next hour, Memona told me about her family and what they practiced in living out their faith. It all sounded reasonable to me.

"Yesterday I asked you who Muhammad was, but you never answered me. You say he was the one who wrote the Qur'an?"

"We believe Muhammad was a prophet, the final prophet sent by God. That is why we do not worship him, but we worship Allah."

"If he was the final prophet—there were others before him?" I asked.

"Oh, yes," said Memona. "There are many men in your Bible we hold as prophets, including, as I said, your Jesus."

"Okay. I'll take these and take a look at them. Now, what say we go get a hamburger or something."

"No, I'm sorry, but I cannot. I must return home."

My heart sank. "I was hoping we could . . . you know, get to know each other better. Can I see you again?"

Memona thought for a moment. "I confess, I do like you, Mr. Quincy. But I am afraid my father would not approve."

"Does he have to know?"

"Let me think about it," said Memona after a moment's pause. "I *will* let you call me again."

Okay, that's better than nothing.

That night I read Rippin's book on what Muslims believed. It was eye-opening. I went to bed determined to take a look at the Qur'an the next day.

CHAPTER TEN
(thirty-five days until the Presidential election)

Muhammad kissed P.J. on the neck, reached around her, and laid a pile of mail on the table.

"Thanks," she said.

She picked up the stack of envelopes and rifled through them. She stopped when she came to one in particular.

"That's strange. No stamp and no return address."

She opened the envelope and removed a sheet of paper and a small note that read: "You have to do something with this. Uncle Willie."

"Who's it from?" asked Muhammad.

"Uncle Willie."

"Uncle Willie? I didn't know you had an uncle."

"He's not actually my uncle. My dad and him served together in the army. I haven't heard from him in . . . wow, I guess ten years or more."

"What's he got to say?"

P.J. picked up the sheet of paper. As she read it to herself her eyes got wider and wider.

"Holy shit!" she exclaimed.

"What? What is it?" asked Muhammad.

"I'm . . . I'm sorry, I . . . I can't let you see it."

"Why not?"

"It's . . . well, trust me—it's better right now if you don't know."

"Why not?" Muhammad asked again. He was starting to get irritated.

"If what Uncle Willie says is true, this could blow the whole election wide open."

"What are you going to do with it?"

"I'm sure there's something to this. But I've got to find out more than what Uncle Willie says."

She stood up. "I'm going for coffee. You want some?"

"Sure," said Muhammad. He watched P.J. as she headed toward the kitchen. He glanced over at the sheet of paper she'd left lying on the table and read the title: "Operation Crusade."

CHAPTER ELEVEN

Madeline James was the one constant in Robert's life of lechery. Most of his sexual encounters were one-night—or morning, or afternoon—stands. On occasion, there would be a repeat encounter or two—as Robert hoped would happen with Kelly Fitzgerald. He and Madeline, however, had been involved in an ongoing affair of more than three years.

As far as his relationship with Wilma was concerned, it had been more than a decade since they had been intimate.

Soon after moving into the White House, Robert had instructed Jamie to procure a prostitute for him for the night.

"I don't want some cheap whore;" Robert told him, "someone with class, with a head on her shoulders."

Jamie found Madeline at what was reputed to be the most high-end escort service in D.C., for a fee of ten thousand dollars a night.

While Robert's dislike for African-Americans was almost as deep as the one he harbored for Muslims, he didn't discriminate when it came to sexual partners. And Madeline, in her early twenties and dark as a moonless desert night, was stunningly beautiful.

She and Robert hit it off right from the beginning, thanks in large part to an exceptional talent Madeline possessed. Robert was fortunate to be blessed with a more than average organ—about three inches more, to be exact. He was both surprised and pleased when Madeline took the whole thing in her mouth, right down to the root.

After that first night, they came to an agreement: Madeline would reserve her services exclusively for Robert; he, in turn, provided her with a three-thousand square foot apartment at the recently built, upscale Oglethorpe Place, more commonly referred to as "The Place," a mere four-minute walk from the White House.

She also received an income of a little over half a million dollars per year and other perks, all of which Robert could readily afford, thanks to his easy access to Wilma's fortune.

While their trysts usually took place in Robert's private suite at the White House, as was the case this night, on rare, night-time occasions, accompanied only by Jamie, Robert would ditch his Secret Service detail and make his way surreptitiously to Madeline's place.

Naked, Robert lay stretched out on the bed, staring at the ceiling, exhausted from two rounds of sex that day, not to mention the stress of learning his own son was running against him in the upcoming election.

He held a glass of bourbon in one hand but was too tired to bring it to his lips.

"That was nice," said Madeline as she emerged from the bathroom, buttoning her blouse.

Robert didn't say anything, but continued to stare at the ceiling.

"Was it good for you?" Madeline asked.

Robert looked at her. "Are you finished?"

"Yes, I'm finished," said Madeline, sounding miffed. "And it took me a hell of a lot longer than it took you."

Robert turned and resumed staring at the ceiling.

"I'm curious about something, Bob. Does your wife know about us?"

"I'd be surprised if she didn't. And it's not Bob—it's Mr. President."

"Well, *Mr. President*, doesn't it bother her?"

Madeline sat down on a chair and slipped on one shoe.

"Doesn't she care you're screwing around on her?"

"I don't know and I don't care. As long as I keep her supplied in clothes and gin I'm pretty sure she's happy."

"I heard about your son," said Madeline, putting on her other shoe. She stood and adjusted her earrings. "I wonder how much it would be worth to him to know about us."

Robert sprang from the bed, the glass of bourbon tumbling to the floor. He grabbed Madeline by the throat and threw her up against the wall.

"Listen, you little shit," he hissed. "You say one word about any of this to anyone and you won't be around long enough to enjoy your next payday. You got that?"

"Ye . . . Yeah, I've got it," replied Madeline, a terrified look on her face. "I . . . I was just kidding."

Robert released his grip. "Get out! Get the fuck out of here!"

Madeline headed toward a door, anxious to make her escape.

"Not that way you idiot!" screamed Robert. "The other door!"

Robert watched as Madeline hurried out. He slipped into a robe lying on the bed, picked the empty glass up off the floor, and poured another drink.

"Jamie," he called out.

"Sir?" said Jamie, entering the room.

"I don't want to see her again."

"Yes, sir, I'll take care of it."

Robert stared at Jamie. "Jamie, what I mean is I *really* don't want to see her again."

"Yes, sir. I know exactly what you mean, sir."

"Tonight," said Robert, as he headed for the bathroom. "Make it happen tonight."

QUINCY'S STORY - CHAPTER IV

My first thought when I woke up the next morning was of Memona.

I pulled on my jeans and the same sweatshirt I'd worn to Richie's for the game, went into the bathroom, splashed some water on my face, and ran a comb through my hair.

Though, to be perfectly honest, there wasn't much to comb. I wore my hair in a style called the 'fade.' Mine was the short variety, but even that didn't sit well with my father who thought we should wear our hair the way God gave it to us.

Easy for him to say: he didn't have that much left.

I found him in the kitchen, drinking coffee, smoking a cigarette, and eating an English muffin.

"What do you got on the muffin?" I asked.

"Nothing."

"No butter? No jelly? No jam?"

"Nope."

I shook my head, walked over to the cabinet, and removed a box of Cheerios.

"No milk," my father said.

I looked at him. "No milk?"

"No milk."

I put the Cheerios back in the cabinet.

"We got muffins," he said.

I shook my head, poured a cup of coffee, and took it into the living room.

I picked up the phone and dialed the number Memona gave me. After ten rings it went to voice mail.

I called six more times that day—and got her voice mail each time. By the time I went to bed that night she still hadn't returned my call.

Too soon? I wondered. Maybe I should be the one to play it cool.

By the time Friday rolled around and I'd called at least a dozen more times, I figured I had seen the last of Memona. Then I heard the phone ring and my father answered it.

"Quincy!" he yelled out. "Phone!"

"Hello?" I said when he handed me the phone.

"Quincy?" came a mellifluous voice from the other end.

"Memona?" I said, not quite believing it could be her.

"Yes, it's me. I'm sorry I didn't return your calls sooner. How is your studying going?"

"My studying?"

"The books I gave you."

"When I didn't hear back from you, I figured you weren't interested so I . . . I haven't really been doing any studying. Although I did read Rippin's book."

"That's a start," said Memona. "I'll be at the library tomorrow morning. You want to meet me there?"

"Sure!" I said. "What time?"

"Ten."

"Okay. See you then."

*****

The next morning when I saw her walk through the door of the library, I swear, my heart skipped a beat.

68

I wasn't a virgin—not by a long shot.

I lost my virginity when I was fifteen. The girl was a year older.

Now, at seventeen, I proudly sported a half-dozen notches in my belt—which was how we kept track of our sexual conquests in my neighborhood. I mean, we actually put a notch in our belt.

Every girl I'd ever met I'd judged on two things: would she go all the way with me and how good a lay was she.

Memona was different.

Sure, I found myself attracted to her—*really* attracted to her!

But there was something about her—call it innocence, purity, decency—that overcame any thoughts or desires I might have had about us jumping right into bed. Instead, the feeling was one of connectedness, of being on the same plane. At the time I had no concept of what the term "soul-mate" meant; now that I'm older I do.

I waved. She came over to my table and sat down.

She smiled, showing a set of gleaming white teeth.

I returned the smile. "I'm glad you called," I said.

We sat and talked and caught each other up on what had happened in the week since we'd last met. It was like sharing my life with my best friend.

Finally, she asked, "Are you still interested in learning about Muslims and our faith?"

I nodded. "Very much."

For the next several hours she answered the questions that had been swirling around in my mind from what I had read in Rippin's book.

I was amazed at how much she knew. She even knew more about Christianity and the Bible than I did. I've always been a pretty good student but, as I said earlier, never attended church and was never interested in anything religious. Now, suddenly, I was.

Over the next several months we got together every Saturday morning at the library. Sometimes we'd talk about what was happening in our lives, but almost always we talked about Memona's faith. She taught me different phrases in Urdu, which she said was the national language of Pakistan. I became somewhat fluent—in a limited way.

She also told me about growing up in Pakistan.

"Women are much better off now than when my mother was young," she said. "Now we have judges and generals in the army who are women. The one I most admire is Benazir Bhuzzo. She was Prime Minister twice. My father did not like her, because she was a woman. I'm afraid he is still quite old-fashioned."

"That's why he wouldn't approve of you seeing me."

Memona nodded. "Yes, he would be much opposed to it."

"And yet, here you are."

"Because I like you, Quincy Bollweber."

I leaned over and kissed her.

She didn't recoil from my kiss. But she didn't kiss me back, either.

She sat back in her chair.

"And I like you, Memona Farooqi."

"I don't think we should do that," she said.

"Why not?" I asked. "You said you liked me."

For a minute she didn't say anything. Then she reached into her bag and pulled out another book and handed it to me.

"Here is a book written by a Muslim. I thought you might find it interesting."

I looked at the title: the *Rubaiyat of Omar Khayyam.*

"What kind of book is it?" I asked.

"Poetry."

I wrinkled my nose. "Poetry? I don't know . . . I'm not much into poetry."

"Give it a try, okay? You might like it."

I sighed. "Okay, I'll try it."

*****

That night at home, I opened the book Memona gave me.

I was enthralled. I was familiar with quatrains from the class I took from Mrs. Gordon, my tenth-grade English teacher.

I had been especially amused when she pointed out that the Humpty Dumpty nursery rhyme was one.

The quatrains in Khayyam's book definitely were not of the Humpty Dumpty variety and I did not presume to understand all of them. What struck me was his seeming fascination with death.

Although I knew nothing about the game of chess, my favorite was number sixty-nine.

> *But helpless Pieces of the Game He plays*
> *Upon this Chequer-board of Nights and Days;*
> *Hither and thither moves, and checks, and slays,*
> *And one by one back in the Closet lays.*

I could hardly wait until the following Saturday to tell Memona how much I enjoyed the book.

*****

I really did want to know more about Pakistan, as Memona described what life was like in her hometown of Zhob. Instead, I found myself tuned out, staring at her, enjoying her face, the twinkle in her eyes, her lilting voice.

"Hey," I said, stopping her short in a sentence.

71

She jerked and looked at me, startled.

"Hey," I said again. "Let's get out of here."

"Get out of here?"

"Yeah, let's go to a movie. You're allowed to go to a movie, aren't you?"

She looked at me, trying to comprehend what I was suggesting.

"Uh, yeah," she said. "I'm allowed to go to a movie; as long as it's not R rated."

"Let's go, then. There's a new one on at the Grand: *Forces of Nature*. Ben Affleck and Sandra Bullock are in it."

"Ooh," said Memona. "I *love* Ben Affleck!"

"Okay, then."

I gathered up all the books and stuffed them into her bag, grabbed her hand and we left.

*****

The movie was pretty good. What I enjoyed best, though, was that she allowed me to hold her hand through it. She even let me kiss her.

It was still light when we left the theater—I knew her father didn't allow her out alone after dark—so I suggested we get a hamburger and milkshake at the restaurant across the street.

She said okay.

After we ordered I tried to take her hand again but she pulled away.

"Not in public," she said.

"Well, can I kiss you?"

Memona thought for a minute, then grinned.

"The next time we're at the theater," she said.

*****

Over the following months, we saw four more movies. And Memona let me kiss her each time. The last time I tried to take it a little farther.

"No," she said, "we cannot do that."

"Memona," I said, "I love you."

She stared at me, a surprised look on her face.

"No, you must not," she said, shaking her head.

"But I do. And you can't tell me you don't have feelings for me."

She hesitated for a moment before speaking. "I do, but it can never be. My father . . ."

"Run away with me," I said. "Let's go to Las Vegas and get married."

She laughed. "Married? Quincy, I do love you. But I am not yet ready for marriage. And I do not think you are either. We are both too young."

"Then will you wait for me?" I asked. "Until both of us are ready?"

"But what about my father?"

"I'll talk with him. I will make him understand. I will convert to Islam if that is what it will take."

"You would do that for me?"

"Memona, I love you. I'd do anything for you."

*****

The following Saturday I waited impatiently at the library for Memona to show. We'd planned on going to see *A Midsummer Night's Dream*.

By eleven o'clock she still hadn't appeared. Using the payphone outside the library, I'd tried calling her cell phone but the calls went straight to voice mail.

At noon I gave up, went home, and called Richie.

"Richie, I need you to do me a favor," I said.

"Sure, Cue, what?"

"I need you to call Faizan and find out what happened with his sister."

"Memona? Why? Why do you want to know about her?"

I shared with Richie that Memona and I had been seeing each other—that we were in love.

"You asshole!" he said. "Don't you know nothing's going to come of that? Her father wouldn't let you near her in a million years."

"I told her I'd convert to Islam if that was what it took," I said.

There was silence on the other end of the line.

Finally, Richie said, "Okay, I'll call him. But I'm afraid you're in for a rude awakening, my friend. It's never going to happen between you and Memona."

Ten minutes later Richie called me back.

"You're not going to like this," he said.

My heart sank.

"Why? What is it?" I asked.

"Memona told her father about the two of you. He blew a gasket. Said he'd see you dead first. Said he'd see *her* dead first. When she told him what you said about becoming a Muslim he got even madder, said Islam wasn't a toy to be played with and even if you did become a Muslim, no nigger was ever going to marry his daughter."

A feeling of dismay coupled with anger swept over me.

"No," I said, "he can't stop us. She'll be old enough in a few years to make her own decision. Then we'll get married."

74

"Not unless you're going to Pakistan to do it."

"What do you mean?"

"That's what Memona told her old man—about being old enough in a few years to make up her own mind. According to Faizan he *really* blew a gasket then. Bottom line is—he shipped her back home to Pakistan to live with her grandmother."

"What?" I shouted into the phone. "He can't do that."

"Apparently he can and he did," said Richie. "She flew out on Wednesday.

"You still there?" he asked when I didn't respond right away.

"Yeah, yeah, I'm still here," I said. "Okay, I gotta go. Thanks."

I hung up the phone and collapsed into the chair next to it.

Memona—gone.

I hated her father.

I hated Muslims.

Except for one.

CHAPTER TWELVE
(thirty-four days until the Presidential election)

Though homicides had been on a downward trend for years, the District of Columbia still ranked as the sixteenth most dangerous of the nation's fifty biggest cities.

So it was no surprise to Molly McPherson and Danny Walters, detectives with the Metropolitan Police Department, to find themselves standing next to a uniformed officer over the dead body of a woman found behind a dumpster in an alley off Atlantic Avenue, in District Six in the southeast part of town. A medical examiner was inspecting the victim.

Some distance away another uniformed office stood next to what appeared to be a homeless man.

"Who found her?" Molly asked the officer at her side.

He jabbed his thumb toward the homeless man. "Jizzbo. Comes by here every morning. Checks to see what he can scrounge from the dumpster."

Danny's nose wrinkled in disgust. "Can he tell us anything?"

"Nah," replied the officer. "Said he didn't see or hear nothing."

"There's bruising on her neck and signs of petechial hemorrhaging," said the medical examiner, getting to her feet.

"My guess is she was strangled, but I won't know for sure until I get her back to the lab."

"Any sign she was sexually assaulted?" asked Molly.

"Nope. She's fully clothed. Looks like it was swift and painless. I guess as painless as it can be when you're getting the life choked out of you."

"Wasn't a robbery," said Danny. "Look at that necklace and those earrings."

"Yeah, and the watch she has on is worth a couple grand," said Molly.

"She looks pretty well-dressed," said Danny.

"I'll say," said Molly. "Those shoes are Miu Miu black leather—worth probably a grand, easy. And I'm guessing the dress is a Gucci."

"How much is that?" asked Danny.

"More than you or I make in a month," said Molly. She turned to the officer. "Purse or billfold?"

"Got a purse *and* a billfold. Couple hundred dollars in it."

"So, not a robbery," said Danny. "Guess somebody just wanted her dead—period. I.D.? Any idea who she is?"

"A hooker," said the officer. "I ran into her once. She works—worked—for Annie Malone."

"Annie Malone? The madam?" said Molly.

"Yeah, I was surprised to see this one here," said the officer. "I mean, look around. A couple cee notes will buy you any action you'd want in this neighborhood." He nodded toward the body. "She was more like a couple grand an hour trick."

"So what was she doing here?" asked Molly.

The officer shrugged. "Good question."

"It's possible she was killed somewhere else and dumped here," said the medical examiner. She removed her gloves and closed her bag.

"Do we have an address?" asked Molly. "And a name?"

"The Place," said the officer.

"The Oglethorpe Place? Over on Sixteenth Street by the White House?" asked Danny.

"That's the one."

"Man, that's a high rent district," said Danny.

"And her name?" asked Molly.

"Madeline," said the officer. "Madeline James."

CHAPTER THIRTEEN

The doorman at Oglethorpe Place looked as though he might have been on loan from the British Royal family.

Dressed in a long, fiery-red frock coat, stiffly starched white shirt, and black tie, he appeared taller than his six-foot three-inch frame, thanks to a silk top hat adorned with a gold band.

He started to stop Molly and Danny from entering when Danny flashed his badge. The doorman nodded, opened the door, and ushered them through.

Inside, the lobby presented an even grander spectacle than had the doorman outside.

Over fifteen thousand square feet, it contained, in addition to the reception desk, a business center, and a fire-colored bar that led into a lounge. Reflected glass with gigantic television sets fitted behind them covered all the walls. The focal point was a free-flowing, glass sculpture that emerged from the middle of the atrium's floor, soaring to within inches of the domed ceiling some three stories above them. Giving the illusion of tendrils, or roots, wrapping themselves around each other, the piece was ablaze with constantly changing hues of red, orange, yellow, and sometimes an occasional bluish-green, that kept climbing, spiraling, upward.

"God, that's beautiful," exclaimed Molly, "like fire shooting up."

"So this is how the rich live," said Danny, taking it all in.

"Yeah, Del and I have a condo on the eighteenth floor," said Molly.

"You wish."

They walked over to the reception desk where a cute little blonde with a squeaky voice greeted them.

"Welcome to Oglethorpe Place. How may I assist you today?"

Molly took out her badge and showed it to the young woman, who appeared duly impressed.

"Police. Oh, my, is something wrong?" she asked.

"I'm Detective McPherson, this is Detective Walters. We'd like to speak to the manager, please."

"That would be Mr. Conrad. Let me buzz him."

Miss Squeaky pushed a button on her phone. "Mr. Conrad, there are two police officers here to see you. Yes, sir."

She looked up at Molly. "If you'll go down toward the business center and take the first door on the left, his receptionist will let you right in."

Moments later Danny and Molly found themselves in Cornel Conrad's office, seated across the desk from him. Though not as opulent as the lobby, it was still a bit larger than the first floor of Danny's home that he shared with his mother and younger sister.

"Mr. Conrad," said Molly, "we're here about one of your tenants—Madeline James."

"Miss James? A fine lady—although technically she's not one of our tenants."

"She's not?" said Danny, looking confused. "We were told she lived here."

"Oh she lives here alright, but she's not a tenant—she's a resident."

"And the difference is . . .?" asked Danny.

"We do have tenants who reside here, who pay rent to do so. Miss James is a resident, but she does not pay us rent. I'm sorry, but what do you mean this *was* where she lived?"

"Her body was found this morning. Miss James is dead," said Molly.

Conrad sat back in his chair, a stunned look on his face.

"Dead? Are you sure?"

"Yep, pretty sure," said Danny. "So if Miss James didn't pay rent, does that mean she owned her place?"

"No," said Conrad. "Miss James's suite is owned by a Swiss company. While I do not know for sure, I believe Miss James lived there rent-free."

"Pretty good deal if you can get it," said Danny.

"What's the name of the company?" asked Molly.

"I believe it is the Kreuzzug Foundation."

"What kind of company is it? What do they do or make?" asked Danny.

"I'm sorry," said Conrad, "but I haven't the faintest idea."

"We'd like to see Miss James's apartment—suite," said Molly.

"I'll take you up myself," said Conrad.

*****

The first thing that caught Molly's and Danny's attention when they entered the suite was a row of windows on the far side of the room that provided an eagle's eye view of the north face of the White House and, beyond, the Washington Monument and Lincoln Memorial. Further on lay the Potomac.

"Wow," said Danny.

"Yeah, wow," echoed Molly. "Miss James lived here by herself?"

"That is correct," said Conrad.

"Okay, thank you," Molly said to Conrad. "We'll take it from here."

Conrad hesitated for a moment, not sure if he should go or stay.

"Like she said," said Danny, "we can take it from here."

Conrad turned and left, closing the door behind him.

"Check the bedroom," said Molly. "I'll take a look around the living room."

Danny no sooner left than Molly heard his excited voice coming from the bedroom. "Holy crap!"

"What is it?" asked Molly, rushing to see.

Danny stood before an open door that revealed a walk-in closet filled with expensive dresses, fur coats, and other pricey garments.

"Look at this," he said.

Molly walked into the room and checked the tags. "These would cost me a month's pay—two months."

At the back of the closet was a second door. Molly opened it to reveal a smaller area with racks that ran from the floor to the ceiling, all filled with shoes.

"My good lord," she said. "How can one woman wear all these clothes? You find anything else?"

"This." Danny led Molly to a dressing table and showed her a small, gold-colored ornate box with an image of the Presidential Seal on the lid.

"What is it?" asked Molly.

"I think this is one of those souvenirs you can buy at the gift shop at the White House. Here, look at this."

Danny opened the box. Inside was the largest pair of diamond earrings either of them had ever seen."

"My, god!" exclaimed Molly. "Those are huge—must have cost a fortune."

"Yeah, but here's what's interesting," said Danny, as he closed the box. "Check the upper right-hand corner."

Molly looked more closely and saw a small, red, Maltese cross.

"What's it mean?" she asked.

"I don't know, but it is kind of strange, isn't it?"

"Keep checking," said Molly. "I'm going back to the living room."

Minutes later Danny emerged from the bedroom. "Find anything," he asked.

"It's what I didn't find. I didn't find a computer. But I did find an iPad."

"Can you unlock it?"

"Shit, I don't even see a home button. I bet this is one of those new models that use touch or facial recognition."

"What if it's facial recognition?" asked Danny. "The gal's dead."

"She still has a face, doesn't she?" said Molly. "We'll take it and let the lab see if they can get in. I did find a calendar."

"Thought you couldn't open her iPad."

"This is a real book, a little calendar book."

"Who doesn't keep their calendar on their computer or iPad?" asked Danny.

"Somebody who doesn't want anyone else to know what they're doing."

"And what is she doing?"

"That's just it—nothing; a manicure appointment every Tuesday, Yoga every morning, a book club once a month."

Danny looked around. One wall was lined with shelves, replete with books. "I guess she liked to read," he said.

"Nothing else out of the ordinary—except this. There's a notation from last night: KT."

"KT? That's all it says?" Danny asked.

"Yeah. And I see, looking back, the same notation about once or twice each month but never on the same day of the week or date. No time given. And, here, this is queer—she has all her other appointments down for the rest of the year. But there's no more KTs after the one last night."

"It'd be interesting to know what KT stands for," said Danny.

"It would be—what . . . or who. Let's check with the manager again before we leave. I want to stop at the bar, too."

Danny looked at his partner with newfound admiration. "Molly, you little devil, you. I didn't think you was that kind of girl. Here it is only nine in the morning and—"

"Oh, shut up you idiot," said Molly. "I'm not going to get a drink. We're going to see if anyone knows anything about our vic. I have a feeling she spent a lot of time in that bar."

"Oh, oh sure, I knew that's what you meant."

"Sure you did. Come on."

CHAPTER FOURTEEN

Molly and Danny sat across the desk from Cornel Conrad.

"Did Miss James have many visitors, guests?" asked Danny.

"None of which I'm aware," said Conrad.

"Did you ever see her with anyone?" asked Molly.

Conrad thought for a moment, then shook his head. "Not that I can recall. She was a very private person. If anyone might know, it would be Dalton, our doorman."

"The guy outside in the getup?" asked Danny.

"If you're referring to the gentlemen outside the main door who is dressed most appropriately for his position;" said Conrad, visibly irritated by Danny's disparagement of his employee, "yes."

"And the bartenders?" asked Molly.

"What about them?" asked Conrad.

"Did Miss James spend much time at the bar?"

"Not during the day, I'm pretty sure. I'm not usually here evenings so I wouldn't know about that."

"Any family?" Danny asked.

"A sister, I believe. I think she had a sister listed as someone to contact in case of emergency." Conrad shifted uncomfortably in his chair. "I suppose I should contact her—tell her her sister's dead."

"No," said Molly, "we'll do it if you'd be so kind as to give us the sister's name and contact information."

"I'll have personnel get it for you. Anything else?"

"Two things. We need to get your security footage for last night. Also, Miss James's calendar had the letters "KT" written in it on yesterday's date. You have any idea what they stand for? Somebody? Something?"

"I'm afraid not. Now let me get that address and phone number for you. And I'll have security send the footage over to you if that's satisfactory."

"That's fine," said Molly. "Danny, why don't you wait here while Mr. Conrad gets us the name and address for Miss James's sister. I'll check the bar and be right back."

Danny was waiting with Conrad outside the latter's office when Molly returned. "Any luck?" he asked.

Molly shook her head. "Tonight. *You'll* check back tonight."

Molly gave the manager her card, then went outside with Danny to question the doorman.

"Miss James? A wonderful person. Quite attractive, too, I might add."

"Did you ever see her with anyone?" asked Molly.

"See her with anyone? You mean here?"

"Here or anywhere," said Danny.

Dalton pursed his lips. "Can't say I have; funny, too, because she's been a resident here for the last three years. You'd think sometime or other I'd have seen her with someone."

"You'd think," said Danny.

Molly handed Dalton her card. "If you think of anything that might be helpful, call me."

"'Course, I don't necessarily see her each time she comes in or leaves."

"You think another doorman might know any more?" asked Danny.

"I can ask him when he comes in and let you know."

Molly and Danny turned to go.

"Although," said Dalton, "he wouldn't see her each time she leaves either since she often uses her private entrance."

The two detectives stopped and turned back.

"Private entrance?" said Molly.

"Yes, Miss James has her own private entrance. Most of the time during the day when she goes out shopping or to the salon or for lunch she'll use the front door, here. But I know in the evening, especially, she uses her private entrance."

Molly looked at Danny. "We need to ask Mr. Conrad about this *private entrance.*"

"Oh, yes," said Conrad, when Molly and Danny appeared before him moments later. "I didn't think to say anything about Miss James's private entrance."

"Can you show us?" asked Molly.

"Sure—right this way."

The trio wended their way through the business center and down several corridors. Eventually they came to a small room that contained two doors: a heavy metal one that appeared to lead outside; and a second serving an elevator.

A keypad next to the outside door was the only other thing in the room.

"This is her private entrance?" asked Danny.

"Yes. This elevator goes directly to her suite."

"Why didn't we see it when we were up there?" asked Molly.

"It's hidden behind panels that appear to cover a window, but actually cover the elevator."

"I don't see any cameras," said Danny, looking around the small enclosure.

"No, there are none. That was done at the direction of the Foundation."

"The Foundation?" said Molly.

"The Kreuzzug Foundation; the one that owns the suite. They had this elevator installed expressly for Miss James's personal use, and specified no cameras, either in here or outside."

Molly and Danny stared at each other.

"What the hell is going on here?" asked Danny. "And who are these people?"

Molly shook her head. "Who has the combination to the panel?" she asked.

"Just Miss James—and, of course, anyone else she might entrust with it."

"Like you?" said Danny.

Conrad blushed. "No, I was not given the combination."

"So you can't take us up in the elevator," said Danny.

"I couldn't even let you out this door," said Conrad.

"Come on Danny, let's go," said Molly.

"Where to?"

"Annie Malone's."

*****

Annie Malone was well known to about everyone in the nation's capital: congressmen, politicians, judges, law enforcement officers, newspapermen, athletes, entertainers, clergymen. All had been clients of hers at one time or another.

Not only did she have an ample selection of beautiful and refined women who worked for her—she also had history on her side.

In 1864, during the Civil War, Annie's great-great-great-great-grandmother, Josephine Boudreau, opened a brothel on

C Street NW, east of 13th Street NW, in an area known as Murder Bay, to accommodate the "needs" of the men of General Joseph Hooker's Army of the Potomac.

Located on the top two floors of a three-story brick building—an apothecary store occupied the main floor—the accommodations were grandiose and flamboyant almost beyond description: cherry red-painted walls, with plush carpet of the same color; glass chandeliers imported from France; overstuffed love seats—red, naturally; and porcelain spittoons strategically placed to ensure there would be no expectorating on the expensive carpet.

Outside on the sidewalk, Josephine's thirteen-year-old son, Cuthbert—Annie's great-great-great-grandfather—served as what in those days was called a "night messenger," directing prospective clients to his mother's establishment.

Over the years the business was passed down from mother to daughter until eventually it ended up in Annie's hands.

It was now known as Empire Escort Service.

Annie's place of business was two blocks and light-years away from that of her distant ancestor's, located on the twelfth floor of a twenty-story, high-rise commercial building which included, as chance would have it, a pharmacy on the ground floor.

The carpet was plush—but not red: steel gray. The walls were painted in muted pastels. The only pictures were scenes of the District.

Not a single spittoon could be seen.

No scantily-clad girls lounging around, either, enticing the customers to sample their wares; in fact, no girls at all. Clients made their choices from photographs and bios sent to them on the internet.

The only person to be seen was Margaret, Annie's receptionist, a matronly woman in her fifties, dressed in a conservative, yet expensive, suit, sitting behind a desk in the outer office from her boss's.

Clearly, she was not one of the women on Annie's staff who provided services.

"May I help you?" she asked, as Molly and Danny came through the doorway.

"We'd like to see Miss Malone," said Molly, flashing her detective's badge.

"May I ask what this is about?"

"Sweetheart," said Danny, "if we wanted to talk with you, we wouldn't have asked for Miss Malone."

Margaret sat back in her chair. A scowl covered her face.

"Please wait; I'll see if she's in," she said, getting to her feet.

"Sweetheart," said Danny. "If you have to go in her office to see if she's in, then she's in."

Pushing past the surprised Margaret, he opened the door and Molly followed.

Annie Malone, a good-looking redhead in her early forties, looked up from her laptop.

"May I help you?" she asked, calmly.

"I'm detective McPherson," said Molly, holding up her shield. "This is detective Walters. We'd like to ask you a few questions about one of your employees."

"Please . . . have a seat," said Annie.

As they sat down, Danny picked up a box from Annie's desk: gold-plated, the Presidential Seal on the lid, and a small, red Maltese cross in one corner.

It was identical to the one in Madeline's apartment.

"Please be careful with that," said Annie. "It's quite valuable."

Danny made a show of carefully setting the box down.

"Madeline James?" said Molly.

Annie looked confused. "Madeline? She used to work for me. But I haven't seen or heard from Madeline in, oh, I guess maybe three years now."

"Do you know who she works for now?" asked Danny.

"I don't think anyone. At least, I haven't heard of it. And I think I would have."

"Why did she leave your employment?" asked Molly.

Annie shook her head. "No idea. One day she was here—the next she was gone. Said she got an offer she couldn't refuse. Wouldn't tell me what it was. Very hush hush. But since I never heard from her after that, I assumed she'd left town. Why are you asking about her?"

"She's dead," said Danny. "Her body was found early this morning over on Atlantic Avenue."

A stricken look crossed Annie's face. "Oh, no," she said. "Dead? How?"

"She was murdered—strangled," said Molly. "She didn't give any hint or warning before she left you?"

"None. She'd had an assignment the night before. The next morning she came in and told me she was leaving."

"Who was she with that night?" asked Molly.

Annie smiled. "Detective, I'm sure you know I can't divulge the names of my clients."

Molly smiled back. "I also know your girls provide more than merely 'escort' services. We're not from vice, so I don't care what kind of business you run. But I have plenty of buddies who do work for vice, and they'd be happy to do me a favor by taking a much closer look at your books. Which, I'm sure you know, they could easily do."

Annie frowned. "We wouldn't want *that*, would we? Give me a minute."

She turned back to her computer and began to type. When she stopped, she squinted at the screen and frowned a second time.

"I'm not going to be able to help you much, I'm afraid," she said. "The transaction was handled through a third party. I don't know who the client was."

"Who was the third party," asked Danny.

"I'm afraid I'm not at liberty to say," said Annie.

"You forget my friends down at vice?" said Molly.

"No. But your friends are no match for my source."

"Why not?" asked Molly.

"Because my source is very powerful," said Annie, sliding the gold-plated box toward Danny.

Danny and Molly looked at each other.

"You're saying . . ." said Danny.

"I'm saying I can say no more," said Annie. "Call your vice friends if you must. I can tell you no more."

Molly stood. Danny followed.

"Thank you for your time," said Molly. "You've been most helpful."

Annie nodded.

Outside on the street, Danny turned to Molly.

"I guess you happened to notice that little box on her desk was like the one we found at the vic's apartment?"

Molly nodded. "I sure did. Somebody at the White House is mixed up in this. And we're going to find out who. Come on," she said, heading for their car. "Let's break the bad news to her sister."

*****

Cicely Townsend's home in the Fort Stanton area of the District was in stark contrast to her sister's apartment.

A three-bedroom condo, it barely served the needs of Cicely and her four children. Sparsely furnished and in sadly need of repair, the unit took up the top floor of a four-story complex.

Danny glanced around the living room. A print of the Virgin Mary hung on one wall. Photographs, mostly children's except for one black and white wedding picture of a young white man and a younger African-American woman, covered another wall.

The only furnishings were a couch, two easy chairs, and a thirty-seven-inch TV. Molly and Danny took the sofa, while Cicely settled into one of the chairs.

She evidenced little shock at the news of her sister's death.

"I'm not surprised," she said. "Okay, maybe I am—surprised it didn't happen before now."

"Were the two of you close?" asked Molly.

"Close. Have you seen her apartment? Look around here. No, we weren't close."

"You knew the line of work she was in?" said Danny.

"Work? Yeah, I guess, if you call flopping down on a bed and letting someone you met five minutes earlier fuck you—if you call that work."

"I take it you didn't approve of her situation," said Molly.

Cicely softened somewhat. "I guess it's not my call to make, is it? I got knocked up by Chad when I was seventeen, and look where I am now."

"Is your husband still in the picture?" asked Molly.

"Hmpff," Cicely snorted. "No, and good riddance."

"I don't suppose you'd know if your sister had any enemies?" said Danny.

Cicely shook her head. "No, like I said, we weren't that close."

"Do you know who was paying for her apartment?" asked Molly.

"Whoever it was, he sure had big bucks. And he sure had Madeline on a tight leash."

"What do you mean?" asked Molly.

"That girl had no life outside that apartment and keeping her sugar daddy happy. She didn't go anywhere, do anything. She managed to stop by here once about a year ago—for twenty minutes; then she said she had to get back before he found out she was gone."

"Can you tell us anything else about her?" asked Danny.

Cicely shrugged. "You probably know as much about her life right now as I do. Sorry, but I can't help you."

*****

"Okay," said Danny, once they were back outside. "That wasn't helpful."

"Except now we have a possible motive," said Molly.

Danny looked at her, his brow furrowed. "Motive? What motive?"

"Let's see who Madeline left everything to in her will—if she had anything to leave, that is."

CHAPTER FIFTEEN
(thirty-three days until the Presidential election)

Molly McPherson and her family—her husband, Del, a mechanic at a local Firestone store; her daughter, Kiki, a sophomore at American University; and her twin sons, Bryan and Ryan, high school seniors—lived in a modest, one hundred and twenty-five-year-old row house located in the middle-class suburb of Dupont Circle.

Mornings in their household were always hectic, bordering on chaos, and this one was no exception. Breakfast was a catch as catch can affair that Del was usually successful in avoiding.

Not today.

"Damn car won't start," he grumbled as he made his way back into the kitchen from the garage.

"You're a mechanic," said Molly, setting three plates of hastily prepared pancakes on the table. "Fix it."

"We have any syrup?" asked Kiki.

"You know where it is," said Molly, gruffly.

"Yeah, I can fix it," said Del. "But it's gonna take time. I'm gonna be late for work again."

Molly looked at him disapprovingly. "This is the third time in four weeks. You're going to get canned if you keep screwing up. Kiki," she said to her daughter who was now back at the table, "you're going to have to take the boys to school."

"Oh, crap," said Kiki. "Not again."

"Can't be helped," said Molly. "Where are those kids, anyway? Del, I need to talk to you—in the den."

"Now?"

"Yes, now. You're going to be late anyway. A few more minutes won't make any difference."

Del shook his head and followed his wife into the den.

"We got another notice yesterday," said Molly.

"What is it this time?"

"We're three months behind on the house. They're not going to let it ride much longer. If you lose your job, we're out on the street. And with the boys scheduled to begin at American next year, I don't know where we're going to get the money for that, either."

A doleful expression covered Del's face as he sat down on a sofa nearly as worn out as he was. "Shit, I don't either."

"Go fix the car," said Molly. "We can talk more tonight."

*****

The Sixth District, out of which Molly worked, provided a sanctuary, a refuge from the chaos of her home. Here, there were no children or husband to deal with—only murderers and the bureaucracy of the Washington D.C. Police Department.

She had finished looking over Madeline James's phone records that another officer had pulled for her yesterday and the security tape sent over from Oglethorpe Place. Now she was checking the woman's financial records.

The girl had been rich.

I should have been a hooker, thought Molly.

One thing bothered her, an anomaly that had her puzzled. She leaned back in her chair, arms crossed, and stared at the pile of papers in front of her. She wasn't conscious of Danny when he sat down at the desk that butted up to hers.

"Daydreaming?" he asked.

Molly looked up. "Huh? Oh, listen, I been going over these Madeline James bank records."

She glanced at her watch: nine a.m. "Glad you could join us."

"Don't forget—I was on assignment last night," said Danny.

Molly looked at him, puzzled.

"At the bar—at The Place. Remember?"

"Uh, huh," said Molly. "What was her name?"

"Oh, I wasn't with—"

"The bartender? Her name?"

Danny grinned. "Mitzi."

"And how long did your investigation take?" asked Molly.

Danny shrugged. "I don't know—three, four hours."

"I hope you found out something."

Danny shook his head. "'Fraid not. Seems our vic stopped in there almost every night, stayed for two or three hours, had a couple of drinks—Cosmopolitans. She'd listen to the music—hey, they have a cool jazz trio there—"

"Yeah, yeah, get on with it."

"Anyway, sometimes she'd dance with one of the other patrons—no one in particular—but she never left with anyone. When she did call it a night, Mitzi said she was pretty sure she went straight to her suite; doesn't seem like she had any kind of social life."

"Was she at the bar the night she was killed?"

"Mitzi said she wasn't. One of the few times."

"So we're nowhere."

Danny nodded. "I'd say so. What've you come up with?"

"There's something strange here in her financials."

"What?"

"First of all, the woman was a frigging millionaire."

"No shit!"

"Yep," said Molly. "She had over a million dollars in her account, and we haven't even looked at her stock portfolio."

"So, what is it that's strange?"

"Every Wednesday ten thousand dollars was deposited into her account from a bank in Switzerland."

"Nice work if you can get it. Or nice non-work, since it doesn't appear she had a job of any kind."

"Here's the weird thing—no deposit was made this Wednesday."

"The day her body was found."

"Right. It's almost like whoever controlled the payments knew she wouldn't be needing this one."

"Like they knew she was dead," said Danny.

"Exactly."

"And I don't suppose we can find out who sent the payments."

"Nope." Molly shook her head. "We already contacted the bank. They cited client privilege. But I'm betting they came from the same foundation that owns the suite where she lived."

"That we also can't get any information on. You get anything from her phone records? Or the iPad?"

"Got the security tape; nothing on it. She got a call Tuesday night. With this damn new technology the caller was blocked. We have no idea where, or who, it came from."

"Yeah, they've made it so even the damn NSA can't get those records anymore."

"And there's no pattern of incoming or outgoing calls," continued Molly, "except to her sister."

"She seemed to take it pretty well when we told her yesterday."

"I don't think they were particularly close."

"For sure not on a financial basis," said Danny.

"But the sis will be now. Seem there's no other family, so if there's no will, little sis is going to get everything."

"Making her the prime suspect."

Molly made a face. "I don't think so—I didn't get that vibe when we talked with her. Besides, her alibi checks out."

"She could have paid someone to do it."

"Possible. But I don't think so."

"And the iPad?"

"Nothing from the lab yet."

"Where does all that leave us then?" asked Danny.

Molly leaned back in her chair and shrugged.

"Your guess is as good as mine."

QUINCY'S STORY - CHAPTER V

I'd been looking forward to my high school graduation for months. Memona had promised she'd be there. That was before her father shipped her off to Pakistan.

Still, my father promised he'd attend, even though he was on duty that day.

"I'll slip away for an hour," he said. "Sarge'll understand."

He fixed our breakfast that morning: pancakes, sausage links, and scrambled eggs.

"You remember to pick up your shirt?" he asked, setting the plate down in front of me.

"I will," I said. I dug into the eggs.

He sat down at the table across from me. "The ceremony's at two?" he asked.

I nodded, my mouth too full to answer.

He sipped his coffee, then asked, "What're you going to be doing 'til then?"

I shrugged. "Just hanging 'round here."

"How 'bout mowing the grass before you go?"

I moaned. We had a big back yard and a push mower.

"No need for a gas mower when we got our own two arms," my father said whenever I brought up the possibility of a new mower.

I loved my father.

In spite of his sense of humor.

After my mother was killed, my father and I became close. Before that, he'd been too busy making a career out of being a cop. But once it was just him and me, he tried to arrange his schedule to spend as much time with me as possible.

Whenever he had to work the night shift, he'd ask Mrs. McWilliams, who lived next door to us to watch me.

Mrs. McWilliams was a widow and as I got older I began to suspect she might be providing services to my father that went beyond babysitting. But I didn't care. She was nice and I knew my dad missed my mother.

My father made it a point to attend every parent/teacher meeting and did his best to attend the few events at school I was in or where parents were invited.

While I like basketball and football, I wasn't good at either sport, or any sport, for that matter, certainly not enough to make the teams at school. He never needed to take me to practices or anything like that.

What I did like—and was pretty good at—was the debate team. Anytime we had a match where spectators were present, my father showed up.

When the time came for me to graduate from high school, I knew he'd be there in the audience.

*****

When I returned home from the cleaners, I went out and mowed the yard. I finished around eleven-thirty, went back inside, and fixed myself a sandwich.

By twelve-thirty I'd showered, shaved, and dressed—all except for my tie.

I never was good at tying a tie; usually, my dad was around to do it for me. But not today.

What the heck; I'm going to have a gown on. Nobody's going to see my tie anyway.

I threw the tie onto the bed, slipped my shoes on, and headed for the school.

Between those of us graduating and our families, the place was packed. I pushed my way through one crowd and caught up with Richie, whom I'd spotted across the room.

"Hey, is your dad here?" asked Richie?

"He will be. He had to work today."

"You coming by afterward?"

Richie's parents were springing for a huge graduation party for him and he had invited me. I suspected their ulterior motive was to keep him from going out celebrating, getting drunk, and killing himself on the highway.

"Probably. I know my dad will have to go right back to work after the ceremony."

"Cool," said Richie, running a brush through his hair. "Come on, we need to get our robes on."

Back in the common area, we scrambled to find our places in the lineup for the processional into the auditorium.

As we processed in to *Pomp and Circumstances* I looked around for my father but I didn't spot him in the crowd.

We settled into our seats and the ceremony got underway.

My row was the second one to approach the steps leading to the stage. As I walked up and started to cross to where Principal Rogers was handing out the diplomas I glanced out at the throng of people who were there to watch their sons and daughters graduate.

Still no sign of my father.

"Quincy Arnold Bollweber," said Mrs. Shoemaker, who was charged with announcing the names of the graduates.

I took the diploma from Mr. Rogers, shook his hand, descended the stairs on the other side of the stage, and returned to my seat.

Where was my father? I wondered.

After the ceremony, I searched the crowd milling around in the common area, but there was still no sign of him.

"Richie," I said, when I ran into him, "have you seen my dad?"

"No, sorry," said Richie as he hurried off to meet up with his girlfriend.

Thirty minutes later the room had emptied out to the point where no more than a handful of people remained.

I went to the coatroom, slipped out of my gown, and headed for my car.

*****

When I rounded the corner at the end of our block I saw a police cruiser parked in front of my house.

Dad's home?

I pulled up, parked behind the cruiser, and got out of the car. Two officers stood on my front porch; neither was my father.

"What's going on?" I asked when I reached the front steps.

"You're Quincy?" asked one of the officers.

"Yes."

"I'm officer Wilton," the officer said. "This is Officer Lewis. Can we come in?"

I nodded, unlocked the front door, and motioned for them to enter.

Once inside, Officer Wilton said I might want to sit down.

From the tone of his voice, I knew something bad had happened to my father. I did as he suggested.

"Quincy, we have some bad news," said Officer Lewis.

"My dad?" I said.

"Yes," said Officer Lewis. "I'm afraid something happened to him."

"Is he in the hospital?" I asked, hoping for the best possible scenario.

Officer Wilton shook his head. "'Fraid not. He's dead, son."

I sat there, stunned. Dead?

"He was responding to a domestic dispute with his partner. Turns out the guy—the husband of the woman getting beat up—was a member of a local Jewish terrorist group. He pulled a gun on your dad and killed him. Then your dad's partner shot and killed the man. I'm sorry, son."

"Listen," said Officer Lewis, "is there anybody we can call? Any family members?"

I shook my head.

"Why don't you come down to the station with us?" said Officer Wilton. "The desk Sergeant will walk you through what you have to do now."

I looked at him, not sure what he meant.

"As far as claiming the body and making funeral arrangements," said Officer Lewis.

*****

I watched the cemetery workers shovel dirt onto my father's casket. The funeral director said I could leave, that there was no reason for me to stay; the workers would take care of everything.

But I stayed anyway.

My father had been with me all the way for the last thirteen years when there were only the two of us. I would be with him until the end.

It was a good funeral. I don't want to say "nice" because there isn't anything nice about your father dying. But it was good.

Reverend Reynolds, pastor of the Baptist church Mrs. McWilliams attended, did his best to make the service as personal as possible but, having never met my father, struggled to do so. Nevertheless, I thought he did an okay job.

In addition to Mrs. McWilliams—who cried a lot more than one might suspect for someone who was just a neighbor—a good number of fellow police officers were there, plus other friends of mine and my father.

But now, here at the cemetery, I stood alone, watching as dirt cascaded down on my father's casket.

*****

Back home, I wandered from room to room, wondering what I'd do now. I'd never thought before about college. I figured I had the grades, but the money that would have been needed was non-existent.

For the last three years, while I was going to school, I'd worked part-time at Gilmore's Dairy. I didn't see that as a lifetime occupation. I'd thought about becoming a cop, like my father. But he'd been violently opposed to it, saying he wanted something better for me.

The house we lived in was a rental. I didn't even know how much the monthly rent was or who we paid it to.

Standing there in the kitchen, drinking a soda, I heard a gunshot outside. I hardly flinched. Gunshots in our neighborhood were an all too often occurrence.

I knew then I had to get out of South Central Los Angeles. I left the house, got in my car, and drove away.

*****

I entered the office, a small one stuck in a storefront between a florist on one side and a neighborhood grocery on the other. A heavy-set man in a uniform sat behind a desk piled high with papers.

He looked up when I entered.

"Hey," he said. "What can I do for you, young man?"

"I want to enlist," I said. "I want to join the army."

*****

For someone who had never been out of California—and only twice out of Los Angeles, both times for debate tournaments—Fort Sill, Oklahoma was like going to a different planet.

For almost three months Staff Sergeant Gordon O'Reilly was like a god to us. Not a benevolent god—more like an overlord. Each one of us in his company felt he held our lives in his hands.

The heat was oppressive. Training was physically and mentally exhausting and lasted from sunup to sundown—and often beyond.

Drilling, marksmanship training, rappelling exercises, engagement skills, field training exercises, conquering the confidence obstacle course, weapons training—including pieces and hand grenades—occupied our every waking moment.

Except the hours when we were on kitchen or latrine duty.

At night we'd fall into our bunks, grateful if we didn't have to get up in the middle of the night to stand watch, but instead getting to sleep through to dawn the next morning, when it started all over again.

It was a joyous day when we finished our basic training, graduated, and received our assignments to our next duty station which, for me, was Ft. Benning, Georgia.

CHAPTER SEVENTEEN

Robert's campaign headquarters was filled with people sitting around, talking, drinking coffee, checking out their iPads—everything but working.

Posters with his face lined the walls. Paraphernalia lay scattered about on the floor and on various desks. Jeans and sweatshirts appeared to be the dress of the day.

When Ivan came through the door, the chatter stopped.

"I guess you've all heard the news," he said, "that Bobby Winslow is the new Democratic candidate."

Ivan held up his hand as the murmuring started up again.

"POTUS wants us to ramp up the campaign. That means more work for all of us—every weekend and lots of nights."

This time the noise was not so much murmuring as groaning and grumbling.

"Yeah, yeah, I know," said Ivan. "Another four and a half weeks and it'll all be over and we'll all get invitations to the inaugural balls."

This brought forth a round of laughter.

"And you heard Frank left the campaign to take another job," Ivan added.

"Who do we have to replace him?" asked Marjorie Pospesel, one of two women who were present.

"One of the best in the business. She should . . ."

Suddenly the outside door opened and everyone turned to look.

". . . be here any minute," continued Ivan. "And here she is now. Folks, I'd like you to meet Lisa Halliburton, our new media strategist."

Lisa, in her mid-fifties, not hard to look at and attired in stiletto heels and a designer business suit, entered the room, eliciting wolf whistles from several of the men.

"Down, boys, down," said Ivan. "Lisa, let me introduce you around: Ed Johns, finance chairperson; George McNamara, my deputy campaign manager; Marjorie Pospesel, our volunteer coordinator; Oren Masterson, who handles our polling; Dave Wilson, communications chief; and—"

"Hi, Wendy," said Lisa.

Ivan was surprised. "You two know each other?"

"Wendy and I go back a long way."

"Okay, let's get to it," said Ivan. "We have a lot of work to do and not a whole lot of time to do it in."

CHAPTER EIGHTEEN

Bobby looked around at the individuals gathered with him in the den of his home: Hank Snow, whom he had agreed to keep on as his campaign manager; Chuck Noble, the deputy campaign manager; Morey Litchfield, the media strategist; Beth Parker, Bobby's chief pollster; and Ku'ualoha.

"I guess this is it, huh?" he said.

"Yep, now it begins," said Hank.

"Where we off to first?" asked Bobby.

"First stop is Orlando; after that, on to Atlanta. In the afternoon we have two stops in Alabama, one in Tuscaloosa and the second in Birmingham."

"I'm booked solid until tomorrow evening?"

"What makes you think you get the evening off?" said Chuck.

"What?"

"Tomorrow evening you're doing a rally in Baton Rouge," said Hank.

Bobby groaned. "Are you kidding me?"

"Hey, we are way behind in this campaign. Don't count on any free time for the next four and a half weeks until after the election. Then you'll have to start putting your administration together."

"Christ, I knew it was going to be hectic;" said Bobby, "but this is ridiculous!"

"If we have any chance of catching up to your dad in this race, we have to use every possible minute we have. Listen, everyone, let us have the room, okay?" said Hank.

Everyone rose, including Bobby.

"Not you, Bobby, you never have to leave the room."

Bobby looked confused, then laughed. "Hell yes, I'm the candidate, aren't I?"

As soon as they were alone, Hank turned to Bobby. "We need to talk about Ku."

Bobby's brow furrowed. "What about Ku?" There was a tinge of defensiveness in his voice.

"Are you going to continue your relationship with him?"

Bobby's face turned red. "A relationship? Hell yes, I'm having a relationship with him. We've been together for eleven years. What do you mean?"

"What I mean is, it's one thing if the two of you were married. It's another if you're just living together."

Bobby's face softened. "You say it's not a problem that we stay together if we're married?"

"Sure. What did you think I meant?"

"I don't know. You think we should get married?"

"If you plan on keeping him in your life. Ever since the furor died down over the Court's ruling in 2015, people don't have any problem anymore with same-sex marriages. Okay, except for the die-hards, like your father.

"But when two people live together and they're not married—and I don't care if it's two men or two women or one of each—there are a lot of people who still can't go along with that. You think Ku would be willing to get married?"

"Willing? In a heartbeat."

"What about you?"

111

Bobby thought for a minute. "Yeah, I think so. I mean, I love the guy. I don't plan on ever having anybody else in my life."

"Then I think you should do it," said Hank, "and the sooner, the better."

CHAPTER NINETEEN
(thirty-two days until the Presidential election)

Annabel Goodwin, Communications Chief for Bobby's campaign, plain, in her mid-forties, would never be mistaken for a beauty queen. But she was smart—she knew how to do her job. She had arranged Bobby's first public appearance to ensure he'd have a receptive crowd.

"Bobby, are you ready?" she asked.

Bobby nodded.

He was in a waiting room at the Orange County Convention Center in Orlando. The room was pleasant enough: a large TV monitor was mounted on one wall; a wet bar extended the length of the opposite wall. The other people present included Hank, Morey, and Abe Opara, the campaign's main volunteer coordinator. They were all waiting for Chuck.

He came through the door, his usual ebullient self.

"I hear congratulations are in order," he said, looking at Bobby.

Bobby looked surprised. "Why, did my dad withdraw?"

"Funny. No, I mean now that you're a married man."

Everyone else in the room except Hank looked as surprised as Bobby.

"You and Ku tie the knot?" asked Abe.

"Yesterday; down at city hall—short and sweet. Like our honeymoon."

"Was your dad your best man?" asked Morey.

The room was swallowed up by laughter.

"No," said Bobby, "Kevin was. And Hank served as Ku's man of honor."

"But Ku didn't come with you on this trip?" said Annabel.

"Thought it best to start out slow," said Hank. "He'll join us in Chicago on Monday."

"Okay, down to business," said Chuck. He looked at Bobby. "We have about twenty minutes before you go out."

"How many out there?" asked Abe.

"I'd estimate a couple thousand," said Chuck.

"Where's Forrester?" asked Bobby.

"He's in his room," said Chuck. "He'll meet you on the stage. Levine will introduce him first, he'll come out, you'll be introduced and you'll come out and join him."

"Who's Levine?" asked Bobby.

"He's our volunteer coordinator here in Orlando."

Bobby shook his head. "I don't like this setup."

"Why not?" asked Hank.

"Wouldn't it would be a good idea for me to meet Forrester first before we get together out there?"

"What do you mean, 'meet him'?" asked Hank.

"I mean, I've never met the guy. I've seen him on TV, but as far as I know, we've never been in the same room before."

"But you met him at the convention," said Hank.

"No, I didn't. I guess he must have been there since he was nominated along with McClaren, but I never met him."

"Shit!" exclaimed Hank. "Chuck, why didn't I know this?"

Chuck shrugged. "I guess because I didn't know it myself."

"Okay," said Hank. "Get Forrester in here—now!"

Tom Forrester, seventy-two, slightly built and a shade under six feet, was a lifetime politician, including four terms as a U.S. Representative from Ohio.

He entered the room, strode quickly across to where Bobby was sitting and extended his hand.

Bobby rose and took it. "Mr. Forrester, it's a pleasure."

"Please, Governor, call me Tom."

"Okay, if you call me Bobby."

"Yes, sir—I mean, okay. It's a pleasure to meet you . . . Bobby."

Bobby gestured toward a chair. "Have a seat."

Forrester sat, followed by Bobby.

"How does it feel to be running for President?" asked Forrester. "And against your dad?"

"Ha! I'm still in shock. *You* should be the one running."

Forrester held up his hands in mock horror. "Not in a million years! I didn't even want to be on the ticket in the first place."

"So I heard," said Bobby.

"I only did it so we could carry Ohio. Otherwise, I'd be back home in Chillicothe right now, raking leaves."

"I for one am *glad* you're on the ticket," said Bobby. "And between the two of us, perhaps we can pull this sucker off."

He gestured toward the wet bar. "You need anything before we go out?"

"No, thanks, I'm good," said Forrester.

"I was pretty much okay with where Senator McClaren stood on all the issues," said Bobby. "But I have no idea where you stand."

"Where I stand isn't important. I'll back you on anything and everything you want."

"I'm happy to hear that. It makes everything a lot simpler."

"I do have one favor to ask," said Forrester.

115

"Sure. What is it?"

"You better not up and die on me before you finish out your first term."

They all laughed.

"I'll try my damnedest not to," said Bobby. "But who knows? It's a crazy world out there. Hell, I may not even make it to the election."

QUINCY'S STORY - CHAPTER VI

The next two years at Fort Benning slipped by quickly. I'd been assigned to office duty, which I found boring beyond extreme. My off time was spent reading and playing catch with my best friend, Shukri, who was Muslim. He made it clear to me from the start he preferred to be called Shoo.

I'd tried to get him to play Euchre or Gin Rummy but he said it was haraam. I asked him what that meant.

"Forbidden."

"Forbidden?" I said. I couldn't believe it. "Why? What's so bad about playing cards?"

"Playing cards does not teach any skill needed for jihad," said Shoo.

"Okay," I said, "now what does 'jihad' mean?"

"It means to struggle, mostly to struggle to live out my faith as best I can."

"I still don't understand what playing cards has to do with it. Is it the gambling aspect?"

"While the gambling is definitely wrong, it doesn't matter if that's part of it or not. Playing cards is a waste of time, time that could be put to better use."

"Doing what?" I asked.

"Praying, reading, sports that keep us healthy, that improve our bodies—things like that."

I shook my head.

"Man, you sure come from a different world than I do," I said.

Which was literally true.

Shoo's family was from Saudi Arabia. His parents had immigrated to the United States in 1979, to Dearborn, Michigan, and he was born the following year.

I asked him why Dearborn?

"There's a big Muslim community there," he said. "A lot of my parents' friends and some of my family from Saudi Arabia live there. It felt like home to them."

I told him about South Central Los Angeles.

He was shocked.

"How could you stand living there with all the crime and killing and everything going on?"

"That's why I left;" I said, "to get away from it."

"And, here you are," said Shoo. "Guess you got your wish, didn't you?"

*****

Saturday evenings, though neither of us drank—okay, I had an occasional beer—Shoo and I drove into Columbus and made the rounds of three or four bars, seeing if we could score with the ladies.

Most of the time, we were successful. While I wasn't much of a looker, Shoo, with his copper-colored skin, jet black hair, and dark eyes, sure was—and a smooth talker to boot.

During the summer months, we'd take in the RedStixx games, a minor league affiliate of the Cleveland Indians. My favorite player was a young shortstop in his first year of organized baseball named Jhonny Peralta.

I also made it a point to visit all the sites on the Black Heritage Trail in Columbus, including both the Porterdale and Old Slave Cemeteries where I'd wander among the tombstones, reading the names and dates of those buried there and wondering how their lives played out.

I decided when I died, I wanted to be buried in Porterdale.

*****

"We going to the game today?"

I looked up from the book I was reading to find Shoo at the foot of my bunk. I laid the book aside and gazed at him.

"I've been thinking about doing something else," I said.

"Oh? What's that?"

"Visit a plantation."

Shoo laughed. Then he knit his brow. "You're serious."

"I am," I said. "You ever hear of the Jarrell Plantation?"

Shoo shook his head.

"It's right outside of Juliette, a couple hours' drive from here."

"Why do you want to go there?" Shoo asked.

"Go get cleaned up," I said. "I'll tell you on the way."

*****

I'd managed to keep the beat-up 1984 Ford Escort my father bought for me when I turned sixteen. Richie's parents let me park it out behind their garage when I left for boot camp, and when I was assigned to Fort Benning I'd flown back to Los Angeles, then drove it back to the base.

At one time it was a bright canary yellow. Now it was about the color of Staff Sergeant Miller's teeth.

But it got Shoo and me where we needed to go.

119

"Okay," said Shoo, as we left the base. "What's with this plantation thing?"

"My family used to live there," I said.

"What? I thought you said your folks came from New York."

"They *did* live in New York. That's where my dad grew up. But they were from Georgia—from the Jarrell Plantation. My great-great-great-great-great-grandfather was taken there as a slave in 1847; he was fifteen. All my family lived on that plantation, first as slaves and later, after the Civil War, as servants, until my grandparents left in1959. That's how my dad got to New York."

"So your ancestors were slaves, huh?"

"Yep. They sure were."

"Mine, too," said Shoo.

I looked at him, thinking I must have misunderstood what he just said. "What?"

"Mine, too," Shoo repeated. "Mine were slaves, too."

"You're Muslim. I didn't know Muslims believed in slavery."

"No, no more, they don't," said Shoo. "But like here in America, slavery was practiced until it was gradually outlawed. My family became free early in the last century."

"So in a way we're sort of brothers," I said.

Shoo smiled. "I guess we are."

*****

I was prepared to find an abandoned plantation, with a few run-down, dilapidated buildings. What I found instead was a well-preserved example of what plantation life had been a hundred years earlier.

The site had been donated to the state in 1974 when the Jarrell family quit farming it. Now it was a beautifully maintained national historical site.

I gazed at the cluster of cabins before us. How long had they been there? Did my father, my grandparents, my ancestors live in one of them? What were their jobs here? It had been a cotton farm; had they picked cotton? Or did they perform some other type of work? Did my grandmother work in the main house. Maybe my grandfather worked with the machinery. I'd never know.

Though my father's parents lived into their sixties—my teens—I never knew them, never even met them. They stayed in New York when my father moved to California. And there was never enough money for us to visit them or them to visit us.

We'd exchange cards and a few letters, but I knew nothing about them or their lives. It was a regret I still carried.

"So this is it," said Shoo.

"I guess it is," I said. While I felt a little bit of connection with the place, it was not nearly what I had anticipated it would be.

"You ready to head back?" asked Shoo.

I nodded.

"Yeah," I said. "I've seen enough."

*****

I was at my desk, typing reports when Lieutenant Reynolds rushed into the office and switched on the TV we kept there to watch whenever the Braves played. Atlanta was in a tight race with the Phillies, three and a half games ahead.

"Have you heard this?" the lieutenant asked. His voice shook.

"What?" I asked. "Heard what?"

I swiveled around in my chair to see what he was talking about. Any thoughts of typing reports quickly vanished as I watched in horror as smoke wafted out from the North Tower of the World Trade Center.

Lieutenant Reynolds and I continued to stare at the screen in disbelief as a second airplane struck the South Tower.

"What the hell's happening?" he cried. "This can't be real!"

"We're being attacked," I said.

"By who? Who the hell's attacking us?"

As unsettling as the images on the TV were, we were completely unprepared for what ensued when first the South Tower collapsed, followed less than thirty minutes later by the North Tower.

Later that day we found out the extent of what happened: in addition to both the North and South Towers collapsing, 7 World Trade Center also went down; the Pentagon was seriously damaged; and a fourth plane crashed in Pennsylvania. Altogether, almost three thousand people lost their lives.

A month later Shoo and I found ourselves, with the rest of our unit, in Afghanistan.

CHAPTER TWENTY
(thirty-one days until the Presidential election)

Sitting in her cubicle, feet propped up on her desk, P.J. was engrossed in reading that day's edition of the paper when Linda Sue, one of the copy editors, approached her.

"Hey, P.J., I heard you were looking for some kind of connection with the White House."

P.J. looked up. "Yeah, I have a hot story, but no way to verify it."

Linda Sue sat down. "I might have just the guy for you."

P.J. laid the paper down. "I'm all ears."

"I ran into this guy last night at the Birmingham Bar. He tried to hit on me, but he wasn't my type."

"Why would I be interested in him?"

"Because he works at the White House."

P.J. sat straight up in her chair, feet on the floor. "No shit! What does he do?"

"You're not going to believe this. He's the personal aide to the President."

"The President? You mean, like *the* President?"

"Okay, that's what he told me; whether it was a pick-up line or not, I don't know. But I thought I'd pass it on to you. Harry might know for sure."

"Harry?"

"Harry Anderson. You know him. He's the White House Correspondent for the paper."

"Okay, I'll check with him. What's this guy look like? Oh, and what was he drinking?"

*****

Harry confirmed what Linda Sue told P.J.: Jamie Inskeep was indeed Robert Winslow's personal aide.

"Don't tell anybody I said this," said Harry, "but the guy is a slimeball."

"What do you mean?"

"I don't trust him as far as I could throw him. First of all, I think he thinks Winslow is the new Messiah. He'll do anything the guy tells him to do."

"But you think he's privy to what goes on in the White House? In the Oval office?"

"Oh, yeah. I'd bet as much as Jackson," said Harry.

"The Chief of Staff?"

"Yep. You got something going?"

"Could be," said P.J. "But I gotta get more information."

"A word of warning—if you get involved with Inskeep, be careful."

P.J. stood and started to leave.

Harry put his hand on her arm. "And I mean, *really* be careful."

*****

That evening P.J. found herself in a booth at the Birmingham Bar.

Before leaving the apartment, she'd slipped into the sexiest dress in her closet, and doused herself with perfume.

Muhammad let out a wolf whistle when she came into the kitchen.

"Mary, Mother of God," he said. "Where are you going?"

"It's work," said P.J., smiling. "Don't worry. I save all my loving for you."

"I guess I shouldn't expect you home early?"

"Not if I'm lucky."

"Lucky? Are you sure . . . ?"

"Don't worry, dear," said P.J. She kissed him on the forehead. "It is strictly business. I'll be home as soon as I can."

*****

Two hours had passed since P.J. settled into her booth at the Birmingham and Jamie still hadn't made an appearance. *I guess I can't expect him to be here every night,* she thought.

She just got up to leave when she saw him enter and head for the bar. She waited a few minutes for him to order and get his drink, then grabbed her purse, laid a bill on the table, and headed his way. She slid onto a stool two spaces away from him.

"What'll you have?" the bartender asked.

"You know how to make a Tequila Ghost?" asked P.J.

Jamie turned and looked at her.

"I should," said the bartender, nodding toward Jamie. "I make one or two—sometimes three—every night for him."

"You're shitting me!" said P.J., turning to look at Jamie.

Jamie raised his glass. "Welcome to the club. Al put it on my tab."

P.J. swiveled on the stool, facing toward Jamie, and crossed her legs, which afforded him a good look at them. She gave him her biggest smile.

"Why, thank you, sir."

"May I join you?" he asked.

"Hell, seeing as how you're paying for the drink, why not?"

Jamie picked up the briefcase at his feet, got up, and moved onto the stool next to P.J. He held out his hand. "Jamie;" he said, "Jamie Inskeep."

P.J. took Jamie's hand but didn't let it go. "My friends call me Cubby."

She didn't want to tell him her real name. The first word that popped into her mind was what she'd been called her first day at the newspaper: Cubby, a nickname for a cub reporter.

"That's it? Just Cubby?"

"Do you need more?"

Jamie shook his head. "Cubby's fine."

"Jamie, what do you do? Besides drink Tequila Ghosts in a bar all alone?"

"My job?"

P.J. nodded and sipped her drink.

"You wouldn't believe me," said Jamie.

"Try me."

"I'm the personal aide to the President."

"What President?"

"*The* President. Robert Winslow—President of the United States of America."

"No way!" said P.J. She let go of his hand and rocked back on her stool. "You're shitting me."

"I told you you wouldn't believe me. But it's true. How about you?"

"I work in a Subway sandwich shop."

"Sounds—"

"Yeah, I know—sounds shitty. But it pays the bills for now until something better comes along."

Jamie smoothed his hair back. "Listen, I have all the makings for Tequila Ghosts at my place. Would you, um, care to see what kind of bartender I make?"

P.J. shrugged. "I don't know. How far is your place?"

"Two blocks."

"Sure. Why not?"

*****

P.J. stood in the foyer, admiring Jamie's expensively furnished apartment located in the Meridian Square Luxury Apartments building. Robert made sure Jamie was generously compensated for his services.

Done all in white—the walls, the ceiling, carpet so deep it seemed if you sank into it you'd never make it back to the surface—the furnishings followed suit: an expansive sofa and three overstuffed chairs, all covered with white, Tuscan leather. The lone art piece was an original Piet Mondrian that hung over the fireplace.

"Wow!" said P.J.

"You like it?"

"Like it? Makes my place look like a dump."

"Fireplace," said Jamie.

P.J. watched in amazement as the fireplace sprang to life with real flames, giving off a warm glow.

"Music," said Jamie.

Soft music filled the room.

"Impressive," said P.J.

"It's Kitaro—New Age Music. We can have something else if you'd prefer."

P.J. shook her head. "No, it's beautiful—very relaxing." She smiled at Jamie. "And very sexy."

"Why don't you make yourself at home?" said Jamie. "I'll fix us a drink."

"I've got a better idea," replied P.J. "You go get comfortable in . . ." she looked around, then pointed, ". . . the bedroom, while I fix our drinks. First, show me where everything is."

Jamie walked into the kitchen, P.J. following behind.

"Everything you'll need is in this cabinet and the refrigerator."

"Okay," said P.J. "Go on now. I'll be there in a minute."

Jamie hurried off to the bedroom.

P.J. removed the bottles of tequila and Pernod from the cupboard, along with a cocktail shaker.

"Good thing I read up on how to make this shitty drink," she mumbled to herself.

"Do you have any glasses chilled?" she shouted.

"In the freezer," came the reply from the bedroom.

P.J. opened the freezer and took out two glasses. She found lemon juice in the refrigerator and proceeded to mix the drinks. Then she took a capsule from her pocket, broke it open over one of the glasses and watched as the powdery contents floated down into the drink and dissipated. She wrapped the empty capsule in a tissue, placed it in her purse to be disposed of later, picked up the drinks, and headed for the bedroom.

Jamie lay on the bed, a sheet covering the lower part of his naked body. P.J. handed him his drink, sat down on the edge of the bed, and raised her glass.

"To an unforgettable evening."

"I'll drink to that," said Jamie, sipping his drink.

"If you're the President's personal aide," said P.J., "you must know all kinds of shit."

"There's not much the President does that I don't know about."

"Yeah? Like what?"

Jamie shook his head. "Can't tell you. Confidential. Top Secret." He took another sip of his drink.

P.J. nodded. "Sure, I understand."

Jamie finished his drink, while P.J. continued to sip hers.

Jamie sighed. "Damn, I can't keep my eyes open."

P.J. got up and fluffed the pillow under his head. "Relax. Take a nap if you want. I'll take a shower and then I'll wake you . . . in a way you'll enjoy, I promise."

Jamie closed his eyes, a peaceful look on his face.

P.J. waited a few minutes, then said, "Jamie? You awake?"

No response.

She took Jamie's empty glass back to the kitchen, washed and dried both glasses, and replaced them in the freezer. Then she returned to the living room, sat down on the sofa, opened Jamie's briefcase that lay on the coffee table, and rifled through folders until one, in particular, caught her eye. She held it up and read the heading: *Operation Crusade*.

She began to read, then abruptly stopped. "Son-of-a-bitch! Uncle Willie was right!"

P.J. grabbed her phone from her purse and proceeded to take pictures of all the pages. When she finished, she rifled through the rest of the contents of the briefcase but found nothing else of any intrest. After she replaced everything, she stood and started toward the door.

I need to make this look like a robbery, she thought.

She turned and walked back to the table where Jamie's wallet lay, opened it, took out all the money, quickly counted it, and whistled.

"Goddamn! There's over five thousand dollars here." She waved the wad of bills toward the bedroom where Jamie still lay unconscious. "You really are a dumb shit, you know that?"

CHAPTER TWENTY-ONE
(thirty days until the Presidential election)

Shenanigan's was not the bar where most of the cops from the Sixth District hung out—which is why Danny could be found there most of the time when not on duty. He wasn't keen on his fellow officers knowing how much he was into his favorite pastime, namely sports—more specifically, betting on sporting events. Twelve huge TV screens afforded all the action he could ask for. And the fact the bar was the base of operations for Danny's bookie, Arnoldo, made it that much easier for Danny to place his bets.

And Danny placed a lot of bets. Most of which he lost, unfortunately.

He sat at the bar nursing a rum and coke, cheering loudly—much to the irritation of the few other patrons there—for LittleTuTu, a seven-thousand-dollar claimer running in the fourth race at Belmont.

"Shit," said Danny, disgustedly, when LittleTuTu finished out of the money.

"I'd say shit, too, if I lost as much as you just did."

Danny turned to find Arnoldo standing behind him.

"Oh, there's always another race," said Danny.

"Maybe not for you."

Danny frowned. "What do you mean?"

"You're into me now for over twenty grand. I'd like to see some of it."

"You know I'm good for it."

"You used to be," said Arnoldo. "Back when you settled up every payday. It's been over a month now since I've seen any jack from you."

"I'll get it. Don't worry about your money. Like I said, I'm good for it. I'll get it."

"You better. 'Cause I'd hate it if you didn't. I mean, I'd *really* hate it."

Danny laid a fifty-dollar bill on the bar and got to his feet. "I gotta go."

"Will I see you tonight?" asked Arnoldo.

"If you'll let me in."

"Sure. You're not playing with my money tonight. Hopefully, you'll win enough to pay me back."

"Let's hope," said Danny.

*****

Danny Walters was better at poker than picking the winning horse or athletic team. That was why he always looked forward to the Sunday night games hosted by Arnoldo in the basement at Shenanigan's.

In addition to Danny, tonight's crowd included most of the other regulars: a retired professional baseball player; a local store owner; a bartender; the priest from St. Angelica's Catholic Church; the widow of the former mayor of Ellicott City, Maryland; a professor from Georgetown University; and Harry Anderson from the Washington Eagle.

Two hours into the game Arnoldo called for a break to allow the players to get up and stretch.

Danny was ahead nearly a thousand dollars.

He was leaning against one wall nursing a beer when Harry approached him.

"I hear you're investigating the Madeline James murder," said Harry.

"Yep. But we're not getting very far."

Normally, Danny didn't discuss ongoing cases outside the department, but he and Harry had been friends ever since Danny and his mother and sister moved to the District from West Virginia some ten years earlier. Harry had helped him with information on numerous occasions, and Danny was happy to reciprocate by giving Harry exclusives whenever possible.

"We know who bought the place she lived in," said Danny, "the same foundation that sent her a paycheck each week."

"Paycheck for what?" asked Harry.

"Nothing, as far as we can determine. She didn't go out much—at least, not as much as anyone might know: she had her own private entrance, no security cameras. And we haven't found anyone who knew her well."

"That's weird. She used to work for Annie Malone, didn't she?"

"Yeah," said Danny. "But not for the last three and a half years, ever since she moved into The Place."

"Let me know if you find out anything, will you?"

"You'll be the first. Hey, Harry, I got a question for you. In her bedroom, there was a little gold-colored box with the Presidential Seal on the lid. I'm thinking of getting my mom one. They sell those at the gift shop at the White House?"

"Not likely. Those are special little trinkets the President gives out to very special people. Was it gold-plated?"

"Gold-plated? I don't know—it was gold-colored."

"Gold-plated. Eighteen-carat gold."

"Eighteen K? That's like . . ."

"Seventy-five percent," said Harry. "I understand he doesn't dole out more than a half dozen a year. You know, people like the King of England, 'Boom Boom' Dimitri—"

"Our quarterback?"

"Yep. Like I said, *very* special people. Did this box have a little red Maltese cross in the corner?"

"Yeah," answered Danny. "What's that mean?"

"The sign of the Knights Templar. You know, the President's a big Knight's Templar fan."

"A templar in the night? What the hell's that? What's a templar?"

"Guess they didn't have many Catholics down in your part of West Virginia, did they?"

Harry proceeded to explain the Knights Templar and the Crusades to Danny, giving him basically the same spiel he'd given Clay Lincoln on Air Force One. "And that's what the Knights Templar are;" he concluded, "the KT."

Danny's eyes lit up as if he'd won the pick-six at Pimlico. "KT?"

"Knights Templar—KT," said Harry.

"Wait 'til Molly hears this," said Danny, grinning.

CHAPTER TWENTY-TWO
(twenty-nine days until the Presidential election)

Molly wasn't used to finding Danny in the office most mornings before nine. And on Mondays, after his standard all-night Sunday poker game, a ten o'clock arrival was not unusual.

So when she arrived at the office at her normal time of eight she was surprised—shocked—to see him at his desk, wearing a grin that stretched from ear to ear.

"I guess you won big at your game last night," she said, hanging her coat on the clothes tree.

"Actually I lost a little," said Danny. His luck had turned sour after the break. "But I did come across some clues."

"Clues to what?" asked Molly.

"The Madeline James murder. At least, I think they might be clues."

He went on to fill Molly in on what Harry had told him.

"Wait a minute," said Molly, when he finished. "You really think there's a White House connection to this?"

"Let's look at what we know. There's a gift box in her bedroom, the same kind given out by one person, and only to special people. Remember, now, Madeline was a hooker."

"A high-priced one," added Molly.

"Yes. And what did the box have on it? A Maltese Cross. A symbol for the Knights Templar. And what were the initials in her calendar for the night she was murdered? KT. And what is his passion in life? The Knights Templar. What does KT stand for? Knights Templar."

"And her private entrance, with no security cameras? Whoever was coming there to meet her—or pick her up."

"Or pick her up," Danny repeated, "and wanted to remain anonymous. And think about this: whoever set her up in her suite and paid her ten grand a week had to be loaded—and I mean, *loaded*."

"But he doesn't have that kind of money," said Molly, "even on his salary."

"Ah, but his wife does. She's worth hundreds of millions."

"So you're saying—"

"I'm saying Robert Winslow, the President of the United States, has to be involved in this somewhere, somehow."

*****

"Are you out of your fucking minds?"

Captain Millard White, head of the Sixth District homicide division, studied the two detectives standing before him.

"Seriously? Robert Winslow—the President of the United States?"

"It all adds up," said Danny.

Captain White shook his head. "What do you want to do? Bring him in for questioning?"

Danny stared down at the floor. Molly looked out the window.

"Guess that could be kind of tough, couldn't it?" said Danny.

"Ya think?" said Captain White.

136

"Okay, look," said Molly. "Assuming Winslow is tied up in this, he's not going to be making all the arrangements himself. He'd have somebody else handle it for him. Who would that be?"

White thought for a moment. "My guess? One of two people: either Jackson—"

"The Chief of Staff," said Molly.

"Yeah. Or that pipsqueak, Jamie Inskeep."

"His personal aide," said Danny. "My bet's on him."

"Where does that leave us?" asked White.

"Bring Inskeep in for questioning?" asked Danny, more a question than a statement.

"You two *are* out of your fucking minds," said Captain White.

Danny and Molly both shrugged.

QUINCY'S STORY - CHAPTER VII

Amidst the cacophony that filled the room in which I was hunkered down, I felt, rather than heard the "thunk, thunk, thunk" of bullets digging into the plastered wall inches above my head. I crouched down further and said a little prayer.

Now, I'm not religious. My father and I never attended church. The closest I ever came to religion was my time with Memona.

But I sure was praying hard this day.

Scarcely twenty minutes after Shoo and I reached the base camp where we'd been assigned, the Taliban had launched an all-out assault.

For someone who lived with the almost daily sound of gunshots for the first eighteen years of my life on East Pear Street in Los Angeles, I was surprised at the sense of fear that washed over me—maybe because those gunshots in Los Angeles hadn't been intended for me.

These were.

I heard the voice of Sergeant Morrissey ring out.

"Everybody okay?"

A chorus of "Yes, Sarge," responded.

"Hang tight," said the Sergeant. "Apaches are on the way."

I knew the Sergeant wasn't talking about Indians, but about the Apache helicopters we used so effectively in fighting the Taliban.

Within minutes I heard the chunka-chunka-chunka of at least three ships as they approached, followed almost immediately by the staccato of M230 chain guns pouring down fire on the fighters who had been firing on us moments before.

Ten minutes later we heard the voice of Sergeant Morrissey again. "All clear."

I straightened up and looked around. Off to my right Shoo was struggling to get to his feet.

"Cue, you okay?" he yelled.

"Yeah," I yelled back. "You?"

"Just some wet pants," he said.

I looked at him. How would his pants get wet? Then it hit me and I broke out laughing.

"It ain't funny," he said, frowning.

"Yeah, it is, kinda," I said, trying to stifle my amusement.

"Come on," he said, "let's get over to the barracks. I need to put some dry pants on."

That was our introduction to combat in Afghanistan. We knew there'd be more to come.

*****

The next day we searched the nearby town, looking for the Taliban fighters who had attacked us. Either they had moved on or they were damn good hiders.

We began a routine of additional unannounced sweeps through the village, sometimes three days in a row, sometimes three or four days between visits.

One evening, after we'd returned to camp and had dinner, I asked Shoo if he wanted to play some catch.

"Can't," he said. "I'm off to prayer."

One thing about Shoo: he liked to pray.

I asked him why he prayed so much.

He looked at me, not seeming to register why I even bothered to ask the question, the answer was so obvious.

"It's my faith," he said, "and my duty."

"It's your *duty* to pray?" I asked.

He nodded.

"I don't understand," I said.

"Salat—"

"Salat?"

"That is what we call our prayers: Salat—it's the second pillar of our faith. Salat al-fajr—which is dawn, just before sunrise; Salat al-auhr—that's midday after the sun passes its highest point; Salat al'asr—later in the afternoon; Salat al-maghrib—right after sunset; and Salat al-'isha—anytime between sunset and midnight."

"Man, that's an awful lot of praying. What do you pray for?"

"The different salats call for specific prayers. Do you not pray?"

I thought back to a few days earlier when I was crouched down by a wall, bullets splattering into the plaster over my head.

"Sometimes. But not always."

"You should try praying always. You might find it helpful. Why don't you come with me—we can pray together."

"I don't believe in your God," I said. "No offense."

"None taken. But do you not believe in *your* God?"

I shrugged.

"If Salat is the second pillar, what's the first?" I asked.

"Shahada—the declaration of faith."

"What's that?"

"There is no God but Allah, and Muhammad is his messenger."

"Muhammad—the prophet."

Shoo looked at me, surprised.

"You know about Muhammad?"

"Sure, Memona told me all about him. He's the one who wrote the Qur'an."

Shoo's eyebrows shot up. "You know about the Qur'an?"

"I even have one."

Now Shoo was bemused.

"Really! You have a Qur'an. Do you read it?"

"I have;" I said, "some of it. Not recently, though."

"What did you think of it?"

"Most of it made sense to me. But I didn't understand all of it."

"You surprise me," said Shoo. "But Memona didn't tell you about Salat?"

"Just that she prayed only with other women and girls, not with males. She would have told me more, but her father sent her off back to Pakistan."

I'd told Shoo earlier all about what had happened.

"Yeah, that was too bad. You sure you don't want to come with me?"

"No, you go do your prayers," I said. "I'm going to take a nap."

*****

I was awakened by the sound of moaning. I raised my head and saw Shoo in the bunk next to me. His eyes were open. The moaning was coming from him.

I stood and walked over to where he lay.

"My God, what happened to you?" I asked.

Bruises covered one side of his face and a trail of blood ran from his temple down to his chin.

He shook his head. "I'm okay," he mumbled.

"Huh, uh. What happened?" I asked again.

"I got beat up."

"Beat up? Who by?"

"Three guys."

"Three guys? Who?"

"Doesn't make any difference," said Shoo, turning away from me.

I walked around to the other side of his bunk and squatted down.

"Who?" I said. "Tell me who. Or why?"

"I'm not sure who," said Shoo. "Why? They called me a towelhead. Does that tell you anything?"

"Because you're Muslim?" I asked. I couldn't believe our own men would beat up a fellow soldier!

"Yes, because I'm Muslim."

"Let's go report it right now."

Shoo shook his head. "No, I'm not going to say anything. It would only make it worse."

"From now on," I said, "we stick together."

*****

I fastened the strap on my helmet and adjusted the backpack I carried. Since we expected to be back in camp by nightfall, it wasn't full. Even so, it weighed over fifty pounds.

It was still dark when we set out. Sergeant Morrissey wanted to get to the town before light so the villagers wouldn't know we were coming. I wasn't sure how successful that strategy was, but he was the guy in charge, not me. Hamra was about four clicks from our base, so it took us less than forty-five minutes to get there.

I was concerned Shoo wasn't with us. The beating he'd taken the night before was worse than he thought. He'd had the medic check him out, and was ordered to go back to bed and stay there.

The town seemed deserted as we entered it, which was normal. On previous visits, there hadn't been much activity either.

But somehow this morning seemed different. It wasn't just that the streets were empty; no lights were visible in any of the windows.

And no noise; only dead silence—until the assault rifles and machine guns opened up. And an RPG hit the lead APC, blasting it to smithereens.

Those who could, ducked behind the two remaining APCs. Others took cover wherever possible. I tried to open a door but it was locked. I kicked it in.

I remember seeing an old man and an old woman backed up against the wall, two rag-tag kids wrapped around their legs. They were staring at something—or someone—behind me.

I turned to look and, for a fleeting moment, found myself face to face with a man, his face wrapped in a shemagh, hiding all but his eyes.

I felt a blow to my head . . . and everything went dark.

CHAPTER TWENTY-THREE
(twenty-three days until the Presidential election)

Six officers on motorcycles led a motorcade of a half-dozen cars, including a limousine flying the Stars and Stripes on the front right fender, and the Flag of the President of the United States on the left.

Thousands of bystanders lined the streets, some waving American flags, others holding up signs protesting the war in Guinea.

Inside the limousine, Robert and Wilma gazed out the windows. Jamie sat across from them, working on his laptop.

"What church is this again?" asked Robert.

"Ebenezer Baptist," said Jamie. "Weird name for a church, isn't it? Who was Ebenezer, anyway?"

"Ebenezer wasn't a person," said Robert. "Ebenezer was an object—comes from First Samuel, when Samuel placed a stone between two cities, Mizpeh and Shen, after he defeated the Philistines."

"So Ebenezer is a stone?" asked Jamie.

"It can be anything that reminds us of God's presence and help." Robert held up his Bible. "*This* is my Ebenezer. It has everything in it I need to know."

Moments later the convoy pulled up at the side door of a large, stone church. Two men approached the presidential limousine, assisted Wilma and Robert out of it, and hurried them into the building.

Several thousand people, almost all of them white, packed the sanctuary. A fifty-plus member choir, garbed in bright, silky robes, sat in four tiers of pews at the rear of the chancel. Above and behind them hung a twenty-foot long wooden cross, suspended from the ceiling some sixty feet above.

The Reverend Elmer Zarian, in his fifties, short and dumpy but spiffily attired in an expensive suit and silk tie, sat in a high-backed, plush chair behind the podium that stood in the middle of the chancel. The final strains of a familiar hymn drifted on the air.

Seated by themselves in the front row, both Robert and Wilma were impressed by the vastness of the room and entranced by the splendor of eight stained-glass windows, four along each of the side walls.

Two secret service agents, flanked on either side by Jamie and Ivan, sat in the pew behind them.

When the singing stopped, the minister rose to his feet and approached the podium.

"Brothers and sisters," he said, the words booming from the speaker system, "today is an auspicious day for Ebenezer Church. As you know, three weeks from Tuesday our country will be electing a new president."

A murmur rippled through the assemblage.

"What I meant to say," said Reverend Zarian, hastily correcting himself, "was that we will be *re-electing* our president."

The sanctuary rang out with applause, shouts, and whistles of agreement.

"Today," Reverend Zarian continued, "it is our great privilege and honor to have not only worshipping with us but also bringing us our message, one of the most God-fearing men ever to hold the highest office of this great country of ours: the honorable Robert W. Winslow, President of the United States."

The congregation rose and a second round of applause filled the room as Robert climbed the stairs to the chancel floor. When he reached the podium, Reverend Zarian embraced him, then returned to his seat.

"First of all, Brother Zarian," said Robert, as he adjusted the microphone to his level, "let me say what a privilege it is for Mrs. Winslow and myself to have this opportunity to worship with you this morning.

"On the way here, Mr. Inskeep, my personal aide, asked me what Ebenezer meant."

Robert held up his Bible. "I explained to him that Ebenezer comes from this good book. I told him this book is my Ebenezer, the solid rock on which my faith is based, the inerrant word of Almighty God, and that I believe with all my heart every word that is written here."

Again, applause and a chorus of "amens" filled the room.

"The Bible is the moral compass by which all God-fearing men must steer their lives," continued Robert. "But there are those who are not God-fearing, who would have us relax our standards to accommodate their deviant and perverted lifestyles."

A chorus of "nos" and "boos" rang out.

"Yes," Robert continued, "regretfully it is so. And I refer explicitly to those who would have us believe homosexuality is not an abomination, but instead something God-given, to those individuals and groups who revel in the unfortunate— nay, I would say, blasphemous—condition our nation now finds itself in, thanks to the injudicious actions of our Supreme Court, wherein we allow the marriages of men to men and women to women."

More "nos" and "boos," louder than before, filled the air.

"I cannot comprehend how these misguided souls—and I'm sure you all know my son is one of those who are so misguided, my same son who is running against me in this election—how they can read this good book and not understand man should not lust after man, nor woman after woman. The great Apostle, Paul, makes it abundantly clear in his letter to the Corinthians."

Robert opened his Bible to a marked page and began to read.

"Know ye not that the unrighteous shall not inherit the kingdom of God? Be not deceived: neither fornicators, nor idolaters, nor adulterers, nor effeminate . . ."

Robert looked up from his Bible.

"Effeminate—which means homosexuals." He continued reading. "Nor effeminate, nor abusers of themselves with mankind, nor thieves, nor covetous, nor drunkards, nor revilers, nor extortioners, shall inherit the kingdom of God."

More applause.

"But Paul was not alone in his condemnation of this despicable action. In Leviticus, we read . . ." Robert turned to the front of the Bible. ". . . thou shalt not lie with mankind as with womankind: it is abomination."

He closed the Bible.

"Brothers and sisters! How can God make it any clearer? Homosexuality is a sin!"

Everyone rose to their feet, applauding amidst shouts of "amen."

Robert lifted his arms. The noise abated and everyone sat down.

"Those two great cities, Sodom and Gomorrah, were destroyed by God because they sinned. And what was their sin? Men lying down with other men. Women lying down with other women."

Robert paused, his gaze sweeping the sanctuary, taking in the assemblage.

"I promise you this. When I am re-elected President, I will do my utmost to ensure this country turns from the footsteps of Sodom and Gomorrah. I will work to reinstate the Defense of Marriage Act and make it even stronger. I will not waiver in this endeavor. I will not allow the morals of our nation to be corrupted by those who wish to impose their deviant lifestyles on us. As God is my witness," shouted Robert, pounding the podium with his fist, "I will not!"

For a second time, the congregation rose to their feet. The sound of applause and affirmations reverberated like thunder throughout the huge chamber.

Robert laid his Bible down on the podium and held up his hands. The noise subsided and, once again, everyone took their seats.

"I asked Brother Zarian to include a special hymn in the service this morning—*God Rest Ye Merry Gentlemen*. I realize we are not yet at the Christmas season, but I had a reason for this. As we sing the words I ask you to pay particular attention to the fifth line in the song: *to save us all from Satan's power*.

"As insidious as that homosexual lifestyle I just talked about is to the moral fiber of our country, there is another, much greater, threat looming on the horizon, a menace that threatens the very existence of our faith , , , of Christianity— and that is the Muslim situation.

"Fellow Christians, I truly do believe *that* is the power of Satan alive and active in our world today. And it must be dealt with."

*****

Christopher Chalmers, host of the popular Sunday morning TV talk show, "The HotSeat," adjusted the microphone hooked over his ear. His guest, Bobby Winslow, sat a few feet away on the other side of a small table. They were finishing up Bobby's interview.

"Governor," said Christopher, "it's been a pleasure having you with us this morning on The HotSeat. I have one last question, and it's of a somewhat personal nature."

"Shoot," said Bobby.

"It's been rumored you have had a number of affairs with other men in your lifetime. Would you care to comment on that?"

"Rumored? Affairs? I don't know you'd call them that. I'm sure you—and, I suspect, every person in America knows—I am gay. It's natural I have dated other men. In fact, before I faced up to my sexuality and came out of the closet, I even dated some women. Did I have sexual relations with all those men? Some, not all.

"For the last eleven years, I've been living with my partner, Ku'ualoha Jordan. Although, now, he's no longer my partner."

Christopher looked surprised. "Oh?"

"No," said Bobby, "He's now my husband—we were married earlier this month."

"Congratulations, Governor!"

"Thanks, Chris. And all I can say is if all of this is fodder for those gossip rags that call themselves newspapers, so be it."

"Governor, once again, it's been a pleasure having you on, and good luck in the upcoming election."

CHAPTER TWENTY-FOUR
(twenty-two days until the Presidential election)

Norman Kunzman had been Robert Winslow's friend since their days together as roommates at the University of Texas. Robert was fresh out of high school, while Norman, seven years older, was a Vietnam veteran attending college on the GI Bill.

Through Robert's meteoric rise in politics, Norman had always served as his right-hand man, first as Chief of Staff when he was a senator; later the same position when he became Governor of Texas; and, until replaced last year by Nate Jackson, in the White House.

Bobby was surprised to hear from him. He was in San Francisco on business, he'd said, and found out Bobby was there for a fundraiser—wanted to know if they could get together for a drink.

In spite of his hectic schedule, Bobby had said yes, and sat now in Norman's hotel room, each of them nursing a glass of scotch.

"It's been a long time," said Norman.

"Yes, it has," said Bobby.

Norman raised his glass. "To old times."

"To old times—and to new and better times," said Bobby, raising his glass.

"I'll drink to that," said Norman, chuckling.

"What are you doing now?" asked Bobby.

"Taking life easy; been down in the Carolinas doing a little fly fishing. When I leave here, Kristine and I are taking off for Hawaii for a month."

"Is Mrs. Kunzman here with you?"

"No, she leaves New York tomorrow morning and flies into L.A. We'll fly out from there."

"You planning to vote before you go?" asked Bobby.

"Yesterday. They let us old farts vote early. You know, in case we don't make it 'til election day."

"To old farts," said Bobby.

Both men raised their glasses again.

"To old farts," said Norman. "Actually, it's the election I wanted to talk to you about. How're your polls coming?"

"You know Beth Parker?" asked Bobby.

Norman nodded.

"She's my chief pollster. Right now it looks like it's neck and neck, with my dad holding a slight edge."

"Sometimes people don't like change, even when they don't like what they have. Can I ask why you decided to run against the old man?"

"I guess the main reason is the Supreme Court. There might be two vacancies there in the next few years. I don't want to see my father get to put his people in. I know you're in my father's camp on that."

"I don't know about that. I think the court's leaning too far to the right now. I'm not sure I'd want to see it go any further."

Norman stood, turned away from Bobby, and took another drink before speaking. "Kid, you have to win this election."

"I'm going to give it my best shot," said Bobby.

"No," said Norman. "I mean, you *must* win this election."

"What do you mean?"

Norman turned back toward Bobby. "Because if you don't, your dad's going to start World War Three."

Bobby looked stunned. "What?"

"You ever wonder why your old man dumped me?"

"Yes," said Bobby. "But knowing him it could have been for any of a dozen wrong reasons."

"Another drink?" asked Norman.

"Am I going to need it?"

Norman took Bobby's glass, walked to the mini-bar, dropped a few ice cubes in each glass, and poured two drinks. He handed Bobby's glass back to him, then sat down.

"He had a good reason, all right," said Norman.

Bobby didn't say anything.

"It was because I knew what he planned to do."

"Planned to do? You mean start World War Three?"

"The war he started in Guinea?" said Norman. "That's only the beginning of it, tip of the iceberg."

"How so?"

"Your dad always was a conservative, especially when it came to religion. In fact, he was fanatical about it."

"Yeah," said Bobby. "I remember how he always used to drag me off to church with him. All that yelling and shouting—it sure wasn't for me."

"The truth is, he hates Muslims. And he doesn't care too much for the Jews, either. He only supports Israel because they oppose the Muslims."

"I don't understand why he hates Muslims so much. Sure, I know practically all the terrorists in the world today are Muslim, but . . ."

"I'll tell you something I'm sure you don't know. When your dad and I were in college, he dated a Muslim girl."

"You're kidding!"

"No. Now, he didn't know she was Muslim. When her three brothers found out about it they grabbed your dad and beat him so bad he was in the hospital for a week. He never forgot that. And he never forgave, either. After he got into office—into the White House—he had those men hunted down. They're now in a federal facility somewhere on some trumped-up charge.

"But that's not all. Did you know a study three years ago showed that Islam is the fastest-growing religion in the world?"

Bobby nodded. "And he wants to stop it by going to war?"

"Not only stop it. He wants to pit the Christian nations of the world against the Muslim nations. He's shooting for nothing short of wiping Islam right off the face of the earth."

"You can't be serious!"

"I am," said Norman. "His exact words were, 'the complete eradication of Islam.' He already has most of the African and Mideast nations involved in this little fracas he started in Guinea. He plans to escalate the war and get Europe and possibly Canada and Australia dragged in on our side. There's even a code name for the whole damned thing— Operation Crusade."

"Operation Crusade?"

"Your father wants to start a Holy War between Christians and Muslims, like back in the Middle Ages. Except this time it would be a worldwide war."

"Jesus Christ! But Congress wouldn't let him do that."

"That's what I thought, too, until I checked around and discovered how many representatives and senators on both sides of the aisle don't think it's such a bad idea. All the terrorist incidents over the last couple of decades have made a lot of them pretty receptive. Half who seem to be leaning that way are doing so from either a religious or national security standpoint. The rest figure that us getting into a full-blown war would be good for the economy, like what happened during World War Two."

"What about the Supreme Court?"

"They'd have nothing to say about it. It would be out of their hands. Even if it was, all the ones on the right are pretty much in lockstep with your dad."

"Who else knows about this?"

"As far as I know, only some of his top military people and Nate and a few others."

"Why don't you go public with what you know?"

"Because your dad would just deny it," said Norman. "He'd accuse me of fabricating the whole thing—sour grapes on my part for being dumped."

"You're saying there's no way to stop him unless I win the election."

Norman nodded.

"And that looks kind of iffy right now," added Bobby.

"There is one way to make sure you win."

"How?"

Norman licked his lips. "What I'm about to tell you only three or four people are aware of, as far as I know, including your dad, your mom, and me."

Norman paused.

"Eighteen years ago your father killed a man."

Bobby almost dropped his drink. "What? I don't believe it!"

"He killed a man. A man who tried to blackmail him."

"Blackmail him over what?"

"An affair," said Norman. "An affair that produced a child."

154

"You're crazy!"

"It's true. I was your dad's closest friend. When he found out from the woman she was pregnant, he had me make arrangements to send her a couple thousand dollars every month for the rest of her life. Twelve years later the woman's husband found out about the whole mess. Your dad was running for governor then. He asked me what I thought he should do. I told him to confess the whole thing, get it out in the open, and take his chances."

"But he didn't."

"No, he'd already decided he wanted to be president, and being governor was the path to get there. He felt the scandal would've ruined any chance he had. He agreed to meet with the guy and asked me to go with him."

"What happened?"

"We got there and the guy was waiting. Your dad got out of the car and walked up to him. They exchanged a few words—I couldn't hear what was said—and then your dad shot him. Just *shot* him! Shot him twice! I couldn't believe it."

"Jesus!"

"Your dad got back in the car. I told him we had to go to the police. He said no, he had no intention of going to jail and since I was involved I better keep my mouth shut. And I did. I've never told another living soul until tonight."

"You said my mother knew?"

"I guess your dad had a twinge of guilt somewhere along the way and told her everything. She asked me if it was true and I told her it was. We never spoke of it again."

"Who was the fourth person?" asked Bobby. "Jackson?"

"I don't think Nate knows. But I have a feeling Jamie Inskeep does."

"Dad's personal aide?"

"Hatchet man is more like it. I wouldn't trust that bastard any more than a three-dollar bill."

"Why are you telling me all this now?"

"So you can use it. Threaten your dad with it, tell him he'll have to drop out of the race and if he doesn't you'll spill it all to the media."

"Why don't you confront him?"

"He knows I'd have to implicate myself if I turned him in. Bobby, I'm seventy-two years old. I'm not ready to spend what few years I have left in jail."

"Even though he'd know I know it's true, what proof would I have to offer?" asked Bobby.

Norman handed him an envelope and a slip of paper.

"Here are copies of checks made out to the same woman over the past ten years up until the time your dad dumped me. I have no doubt the payments are still being made. And here's her name and address."

Bobby took the slip of paper and read it: *Alice O'Shea, 1441 Jenson Road, Ivy City*

CHAPTER TWENTY-FIVE

Hank jumped up out of his chair, nearly knocking over the lamp.

"Get out of town! Are you shitting me? Your old man knocked off somebody?"

"According to Norman," said Bobby.

"And you believe him?"

"I've known Norman a long time . . . all my life. I don't think he'd lie about something like this, not even to get back at my dad."

"God, this is huge. What are you going to do?"

Bobby's hands flew up in frustration. "Shit, I don't know."

"You know, this would sew up the election for you."

"That's what Norman said. It would also put my father in jail. I don't know if I could do that."

"Ha! I bet he'd do it to you in a heartbeat if the situation was reversed."

"Maybe. I don't know. But I do know what I need to do first."

"What's that?"

"Make a phone call."

*****

Wilma lay stretched out on the bed, her eyes focused on a spider crawling on the ceiling. She was beginning to think she was too old to go on these campaign trips with Robert. Whereas they seemed to invigorate, energize him, they exhausted her.

And, besides, she wasn't all that gregarious. She didn't relish meeting people, shaking hands, having tea, listening to people give speeches—especially Robert. And she and Robert had come to an agreement long ago that she would not need to give speeches. In fact Robert made it clear he didn't want her doing them.

Why was she even along? At least in the privacy of the White House, she could get as shit-faced drunk as she wanted to. Out here on the road, she had to watch herself, drink moderately—what, for her, passed as moderately—and not make a total spectacle of herself.

Deep down, though she would never admit it to anyone, especially Robert, she hoped he'd lose the election. Perhaps they'd move back to Texas or Louisiana and live somewhat more normal lives. At least she could. She knew Robert could never give up the limelight.

The ringing of the telephone brought her out of her reverie. She wondered who it could be. Robert was particular about whose calls he allowed to come through. She picked up the receiver.

"Hello," she said, slurring her words.

She was surprised and delighted to hear her son's voice on the other end.

"Mom?"

Wilma sat up on the bed. "Bobby? Oh, Honey, it's so good to hear your voice. How are you?"

"I'm fine, Mom."

"Do you think we could get together? Meet for a drink somewhere?"

"You're in Kansas City, Mom. I'm in San Francisco. I don't think it would be too practical."

"Oh, no, I guess you're right," said Wilma.

"Mom, I have a question to ask you. It's something I heard about Dad."

*****

Wilma sat, nervously kneading her hands.

Robert loomed over her, his face a crimson red.

"He knows? How the hell can he know?" Robert shouted.

Wilma shrank back. "I don't know, dear."

"I do," said Robert, pacing back and forth. "It was that damned Norman. I never did trust that son-of-a-bitch."

"But, dear, he was your best friend."

"*Was* is the key word there. I knew I should have done more than just fire his ass."

"Yes, dear."

Robert looked at Wilma. "What else did he say?"

Wilma looked confused. "What? Who?"

"Bobby," said Robert, impatiently. "What else did he say?"

"Nothing, dear."

Robert waved his hand. "Why don't you go fix yourself a drink? And tell Jamie to get his ass in here—now!"

Wilma hurried from the room, glad to be out of range of Robert's wrath.

Moments later Jamie entered.

"Bobby knows," said Robert.

Now it was Jamie's turn to look confused. "Bobby knows? Knows what?"

"The O'Shea thing. He knows about the O'Shea thing."

"You mean the money?"

"No," said Robert, getting angrier by the minute. "He knows what I did to the bastard."

"Jesus," exclaimed Jamie, sitting down.

Robert glowered at him and he sprang to his feet.

"Sorry, sir. It just slipped out," said Jamie.

Robert waved his hand dismissively. "Forget it. Sit down, sit down."

"How did he find out?" asked Jamie.

"I'm pretty sure it was Kunzman. He's the only one who knew about it," Robert stopped pacing and stared at Jamie, "besides you and Wilma."

Jamie jumped up from his chair.

"No, sir, swear to God! I haven't told anyone."

"Okay, well, that's neither here nor there right now. The question is, what are we going to do about it?"

"Has Bobby contacted you?"

"Not yet."

"Do you think he'd use it? Make it public?"

"I don't know," said Robert, "hard to tell what the little queer will do."

"There is one way to make sure he doesn't let it get out."

Robert stared hard at Jamie. "You're not thinking what I think you're thinking, are you?"

"Sir, I realize he's your son. But there comes a time when the good of the nation—of the whole Christian world—overcomes family loyalty."

"He is my son . . . even if he is a cock-sucking queer." Robert sat down and ran his hand over his forehead, brushing his hair back. "I'm not going to do anything—not yet, anyway. Let's wait and see if he contacts me. I'm pretty sure he wouldn't go public without talking to me first. In the meantime, I want to make sure Norman doesn't talk to anyone else."

"How do you want me to handle it, sir?"

Robert's eyes met Jamie's. "Permanently."

*****

Norman was surprised when he looked through the peephole of his hotel room door. It was after eleven—he was expecting room service. Instead, two men in dark suits stood in the hallway.

"What do you want?" asked Norman.

"F.B.I.," one of the men replied.

"Some identification, please," said Norman.

The man held his identification up to the peephole.

Norman unlocked the door and swung it open.

"Sir, we need you to come with us," the man said.

"Where are we going?"

"It's a matter of national security. We'll explain on the way."

CHAPTER TWENTY-SIX
(twenty days until the Presidential election)

Dressed only in a bathrobe, Bobby sat at a small table in his hotel room, eating his morning grapefruit while he watched the local news.

An attractive female was giving the local weather conditions when she stopped, put her hand against her ear, listening.

"We have some breaking news," she said, removing the hand. "It appears that Norman Kunzman—"

Bobby's spoon stopped halfway to his mouth.

"—former Chief of Staff to President Robert Winslow, has apparently committed suicide. Harry Moore will now bring you more of the story."

Bobby sat back in the chair, spoon still poised in mid-air, a shocked expression covering his face as Moore appeared on the screen.

"Police speculate Mr. Kunzman somehow gained entry to the twenty-second-floor observation tower of the Chalmers Building and jumped to his death from there," said the newsman.

The spoon fell from Bobby's hand as he jumped up from his chair.

"No fucking way!" he exclaimed.

"A note was found in Kunzman's hotel room indicating he was still depressed over his removal as President Winslow's Chief of Staff last year. We'll bring you additional . . ."

Bobby grabbed the phone and punched in numbers as the newscaster droned on in the background. "Hank, I need you in here right now."

"I just heard," said Hank. "I'm on my way."

Moments later Hank sat in Bobby's hotel room.

"This is bullshit!" said Bobby. "There's no way Norman killed himself. He told me last night he and Mrs. Kunzman were leaving today for Hawaii."

"You think . . ." Hank hesitated. "You think your dad had something to do with Kunzman's death?"

"Before last night I would have said 'no way.' I mean, he's bigoted and manipulative . . . and a real son-of-a-bitch. But . . . a murderer? I don't want to believe he had anything to do with it. But, now . . . well, to tell you the truth—after I know what he did eighteen years ago—I wouldn't be surprised."

"When you talked to your mother about O'Shea, did you also tell her what Kunzman told you about Operation Crusade?" asked Hank.

"No. I doubted she would have known anything about it, and she didn't have to."

"What are you going to do?" asked Hank.

"Before this, I wanted to win the election."

"And now?"

"And now," said Bobby, nodding, "I'm determined to win it; whatever I have to do."

QUINCY'S STORY - CHAPTER VIII

My eyes struggled to open. When they did, everything was blurry, as if I were under water.

I was sitting in a chair; that much I knew. When I tried to move my arms and legs I discovered I was restrained.

Slowly, the vision of a man came into focus, a man sitting about four feet away from me. The back of his chair faced me, the man's arms draped over it. His skin was dark, his beard long, and around his head he wore a turban, the type worn by Taliban fighters. I shook my head in an attempt to clear it. I shut my eyes and when I opened them again the man came into clearer view. He was in his late twenties or early thirties, I figured.

"Welcome back," the man said in perfect English. He spoke with a British accent—not what I expected.

"Where am I?" I asked. Though I knew without any doubt I'd been captured.

"You are with us," the man said. "And we are where we need to be. What is your name?"

I looked at him and took a deep breath before I answered. "Bollweber; Quincy; corporal; April 26, 1981; four, nine, seven, eight, two, one, six, two, three."

The man smiled, showing an almost perfect set of glistening white teeth.

"And I know what regiment you are with," he said, "so that information is not necessary. Why are you here, corporal Bollweber?"

I didn't understand; why was I here?

"I'm here because you brought me here—wherever here is."

"No, corporal, I mean why are you here in Afghanistan? This is not your country, no?"

I twisted my wrists, testing how securely I was bound. There was no give.

"I'm here serving my country," I said, resigned the ropes weren't going anywhere. "It's my duty."

"Your duty, eh? To come into *my* country and wage war against me and my men—my people?"

"Against terrorists. Like the ones that brought down our towers."

The man nodded. "A great day, was it not? So you come here hunting for us to kill us all for revenge?"

"You're damned right!" I said, my eyes fixed on his.

"And where did you learn to speak Urdu?" the man asked.

"What?"

"Urdu. You mumbled a few phrases in Urdu while you were unconscious. Where did you learn to speak it?"

"Under the terms of the Geneva Convention, I don't have to tell you anything more than what I've already told you."

"Ah, yes," said the man, smiling. "But then, what kind of conversation could we have?"

"Let me ask you a question," I said. "Where did you learn to speak English?"

The man's face beamed.

"Oxford. I studied there. Political Science. Who is Memona?"

Memona? How did he know about her?

"You mentioned her when you were unconscious," said the man, as if he were reading my mind. "Never mind. Are you hungry?"

Again, I was taken aback. Was I hungry? I was expecting to get beaten up or, at worst, beheaded. But was I *hungry*?

"No," I answered, "I'm not hungry. But I could use a drink of water."

"Okay," said the man. He stood, walked over to a table, poured a glass of water from a pitcher, returned, and held the glass to my lips.

Greedily I drank from it.

"Enough?" he asked.

I nodded.

He took the glass back to the table, then pulled his chair up closer to me and sat down.

"Now," he said, taking a handgun from the holster at his waist and placing the barrel on my forehead, "where did you learn to speak Urdu, and who is Memona?"

I hesitated a second before answering, long enough to realize that giving him that small piece of information was better than getting a bullet in my brain.

"My girlfriend," I said, "Memona. She was from Pakistan. She taught me what Urdu I know."

The man pulled the gun back. "See how much better we can communicate when you answer my questions? And where is Memona now? Waiting for you back in America?"

"Her father sent her back to Pakistan. I haven't seen or heard from her in years."

"She is Muslim."

"Yes."

"Do you know the Qur'an?"

I hesitated. How much should I tell him?

I nodded. "Memona introduced me to it."

"Have you read it?"

"Some."

"But you are not Muslim. Are you Christian?"

"I believe in God. But I don't go to any church."

"Do you believe in Allah?"

"My friend says God and Allah are the same."

"Your friend? Who is your friend?"

Once again I hesitated. Should I tell him? I finally decided I should—for my own safety.

"Shoo—Shukri."

"Your friend is Muslim?"

"Yes."

"Your friend is a Muslim and your girlfriend is Muslim. Yet here you are, trying to kill Muslims."

"Terrorists," I said. "I'm trying to kill terrorists—like you."

The man's face tightened and his eyes burned into mine.

"We are not terrorists," he said. "We are soldiers of Allah. Our war is against the Christian-Jewish alliance that seeks to wipe Islam from the face of this earth. It is our duty to rid our land of the infidels who have invaded us. Only when they are gone and our country is once again under our control will we cease fighting. You should understand."

"Why should I understand?" I asked.

"Because of who you are—what you are: your race. The white man has been subject over you ever since the first African met the first European. And in your America, especially, this has been your fate in life. Your country was built on slavery."

"I'm not a slave," I said as I felt the anger rise in me. "I'm a free man. We don't have slaves in the United States anymore."

The man laughed. "Perhaps you do not see it," he said. "But every black person in America is a slave to the dictates of the white man."

"Like your women," I said.

"Our women?"

"You treat your women like slaves."

The man's face tightened again. "If women were meant to be equal to men, Allah would have created them so. He did not. They are not as strong as men, they are not as intelligent as men, they do not know how to govern like men. It is a man's duty to protect his wife and provide for her. It is a wife's duty to take care of the home and do what her husband tells her to do."

"And you don't call that slavery?" I asked.

The man rose from his chair. "Enough talk for now. We shall continue our conversation tomorrow."

As the man started to leave I blurted out, "You know my name—what's yours?"

"Haaziq," said the man. "I am Haaziq Azzam."

*****

I was taken to a small room, no more than six by six. Along one wall was a sleeping mat. A metal bucket sat in one corner. A single small window on the back wall was too high for me to see out of. A wooden door held a small opening covered on the outside by a metal plate.

I wondered if any other prisoners were being held here. And where was here? I had no idea.

Exhausted, I sank onto the mat and within minutes was fast asleep.

*****

Early the next morning the panel on the door slid open and a hand thrust through holding a tray on which sat a small bowl.

I took the bowl and retreated to the mat where I ravenously consumed its contents, wondering what it was I was eating.

Later that day, about the time the sun disappeared from the window, the door opened and a man beckoned for me to emerge.

Along with a second man he escorted me to the same room I'd been in the day before, indicated for me to sit down, and tied me in the chair.

Minutes later Haaziq entered.

"How did you sleep?" he asked as he slid onto his chair.

"It's not exactly the Biltmore," I said.

"No, you're right—it is not. I have stayed at Biltmores. You have stayed at a Biltmore?"

"Not hardly," I said. "But I've stayed in some built less."

Haaziq grinned. "A sense of humor; I like that. Now then, what shall we talk about today?"

"You can talk about anything you want. I've said all I'm going to say."

"I see. Then let me tell you about me—one of my favorite subjects."

For the next hour, Haaziq poured out his life story. Born in Syria to a Sunni family, his father an executive in a large oil company, he was educated at Oxford, then returned home and eventually became a member of the People's Council. He married his childhood sweetheart who bore him three children, two boys, and one girl.

He had heard Osama Bin Laden speak and came to accept his ideology and hatred of America. A week after 9/11 he left his family in Syria, traveled to Afghanistan, and joined the Taliban. Now he was a commander of the men under his control.

"And that is me," he finished. "Now, are you sure you don't want to tell me about you?"

I didn't say anything.

"Then let me tell you what I think. I think being a Negro you have been under the white man's thumb your entire life. You are probably intelligent enough to be an officer; yet here you are—a lowly enlisted man.

"You came from a poor neighborhood—Chicago, perhaps? Your father struggled all his life to provide for you and your family. You were either drafted—because you couldn't get a deferment; after all, you're not college material, they would tell you—or you enlisted to get out of the life you were in."

As Haaziq spoke, images flashed through my mind: all the times I'd been hassled by white cops; my father's body in his casket after having been killed by a Jewish Nationalist; Rodney King; Muhammad Ali, O. J. Simpson—all blacks who, like me, had been harassed by white men, only worse. And then there was Shoo, who, just days ago, was beaten by his fellow soldiers—white soldiers—because he was Muslim.

But the image that stuck most in my mind was looking out at the fields at the Jarrell Plantation and realizing my ancestors worked those fields as slaves. Had I been alive two hundred years ago, it could have been me out there in those fields.

As I remembered that scene, I almost felt like I was out in those fields, slaving away, picking cotton, with no hope of ever being free.

Then I remembered watching on TV as thousands of people were killed when the twin towers came down.

That was what this man who sat here before me believed in: death to all infidels.

I admit: I was conflicted.

*****

Over the next week, I tried twice to escape. On neither occasion did I make it out of the building. Both times I was beaten when they caught me.

"Why do you try to escape?" asked Haaziq after my second attempt. "Do you not like it here? Do we not treat you well?"

"Why haven't you tortured me like you do other prisoners?" I asked. "Why haven't you killed me? I've seen the pictures of the men you've beheaded. Why not me?"

"First of all," said Haaziq, "you have not seen me behead anyone. That is barbaric. I prefer a simple shot to the head. Besides, you are special. I see something in you."

"You see something in me? What? What do you see in me?"

"I see a Muslim."

I laughed.

"A Muslim? You see a Muslim in me? You're out of your friggin' mind!"

Haaziq smiled.

"You have suffered the same injustices, the same prejudices my people have. The difference is you have not yet given your heart, your life, your allegiance, to Allah. Once you do that, you will find new meaning for your life."

"You're crazy," I said. "What makes you think I'd ever become a Muslim?"

"I believe you already have in a sense," said Haaziq. "Through your relationships with your girlfriend and your

171

friend, Shukri, and your reading of the Qur'an you know our faith is pure, and our beliefs are good, they are righteous. And once you see we fight not as terrorists, but as mujahedeen, holy warriors, for our country and for Allah, you will join us in our struggle. I know this as surely as you sit here before me now."

Before I could say anything he got up.

"We shall talk again tomorrow," he added as he walked from the room.

Back in my room, I thought about what Haaziq said.

He was wrong. I would never become a Muslim.

*****

Over the next month Haaziq and I talked every day but one—a day on which, I discovered later, he and his men had gone on a raid. Sometimes our discussions lasted no more than thirty minutes, other times four to five hours.

Little by little, I opened up. We shared our life stories, laughing at the ridiculous choices we each had made as teenagers, commiserating together on the tragedies we'd undergone. He read to me from the Qur'an, sharing his interpretation of the scriptures. I was no longer being tied to the chair.

Haaziq continued to question me about my unit, but I refused to give him any information. Oddly enough, he seemed to accept I wouldn't, even though I was prepared each day for him to change his mind and have me tortured. How long I could hold out, I wasn't sure.

I found myself praying, something that had never been a part of my life. Whether it was my situation or the depth of faith in Allah that I saw in Haaziq, I wasn't sure.

I knew I couldn't continue in my current state indefinitely.

I had to make a decision.

QUINCY'S STORY - CHAPTER IX

I watched Haaziq settle into his chair across from me.

"I'm ready to join up with you," I said before he had a chance to speak.

For a minute he didn't say anything.

"Join up with me?" he said finally.

"With your men. To fight with you."

"Why would you want to do that?"

"Because you've convinced me that your fight is the right one."

"My followers are all Muslim," said Haaziq.

"I will become Muslim," I said.

"Again, why would you?"

"I believe it is the one true religion. I've seen how Memona and Shoo are . . . I don't know—committed? How committed they are? And everything you have said to me makes sense. I am ready. I am ready to accept Allah as my God. Besides, you said yourself that I am a Muslim."

"And how can I know what you say is true?" asked Haaziq.

I told him everything I could about my unit, although I wasn't sure it was all still relevant since I had been gone from it for almost a month.

"What is the first pillar of Islam?" Haaziq asked.

"There is no god but Allah. Muhammad is the messenger of Allah."

"And do you believe that?"

"I do," I said.

"Come with me," said Haaziq.

He led me to a small room where several rolled-up prayer rugs rested in one corner. Unlike my cell and the room where the two of us had been meeting, the walls were painted a gleaming white, and the floorboards appeared clean enough that you could eat off of them. A small window on one wall let in a shaft of sunlight.

"Take a mat and lay it out on the floor," said Haaziq.

I did as he said.

"Turn it about fifteen degrees to the right," he said.

Again, I followed his order.

"Why that direction?" I asked

"Because that is the direction of Mecca."

"How do you know which direction Mecca is?"

"Come, look at this," he said.

I followed him as he went to the wall where a large map of the Middle East hung.

"This is Mecca," he said. He pointed to a spot on the map about halfway down the coast of Saudia Arabia and a short distance from the Red Sea. "And here is where we are."

He pointed to another spot in Afghanistan, some distance from where my unit was stationed when I was captured. I wondered if they were still there.

"And so," said Haaziq, taking his finger and drawing an imaginary line from the last point to the former one, "this is the direction Mecca is in. What direction is that in this room?"

"The direction you have the mat pointed in," I answered.

"Yes."

"But what if you weren't sure where you were? How do you know which direction then?"

"You use this," said Haaziq. He pulled a small round object from his pocket.

"A compass?" I said.

"A Qibla compass. It is designed specifically to show how to find the correct direction to Mecca."

Haaziq held the instrument out so I could see it and explained how it worked.

Pretty ingenious.

Haaziq took a second mat and laid it down next to the first one.

"Remove your shoes," he said, "and stand on the mat facing toward the niche at the top."

For the next thirty minutes, Haaziq instructed me on how to pray, when to pray, what position I should use, what I should say.

"I'm not sure I can remember all that," I said.

"You will learn. But do you have any questions now?"

"Yeah," I said. "Can I get my piece back?"

"You are ready to go out and kill the men with whom you served until a few weeks ago?"

"Protection," I said. "I want to be able to shoot back if somebody's shooting at me."

"Not right now," said Haaziq, "perhaps in a week. You have much yet to learn, grasshopper."

I laughed. "You've seen The Karate Kid," I said.

He smiled. "One of my favorite movies. I think it is time for you to meet the rest of my men. Your time as my prisoner has come to an end."

*****

Over the next week, I got to know the rest of Haaziq's fighters, about forty in all. Previously, the only one I'd known was the one who brought my food and escorted me to the room where I met with Haaziq. He'd never spoken. I had the feeling none of them trusted me. The feeling was mutual.

I discovered I was the only one who had been captured in the raid; there were no other prisoners.

Every day, Haaziq joined me in the prayer room as he continued to instruct me on how to pray properly as well as other matters he felt I should know.

At the end of the week, I met with him again in the little room where we had been meeting before I told him I wanted to join with him.

"The time has come," he said.

"I'm getting my piece back?"

"No, it will not be returned to you."

I frowned. "Why not? How will I defend myself if we get attacked?"

"You will not be here. I am sending you back to your unit."

I was confused. "Sending me back? I don't understand."

"I have many recruits I can draw from to fill my ranks. They come from all over and are experienced fighters who have seen much action. Have you ever killed anyone, Quincy?"

I hesitated before answering.

"I don't know . . . maybe. In the firefights, I fired at the flashes of light. I don't know if I ever hit anyone."

"That is what I suspected," said Haaziq. "But you still can be of great value to me. Even more so than these men I now command."

"How?"

"You will go back to your unit. You will be an American soldier again. Then, sometime in the future, you will be asked to do something that will benefit our cause."

"You want me to be a spy," I said.

"Perhaps," said Haaziq. "We must see what the future will bring."

"When do I go?"

"Tomorrow. In the morning we will drop you off two miles from where your men are."

"You know where they are?"

"We always know where they are."

*****

Early the next morning they drove me out to the spot where I was to be let off. Haaziq and three other men accompanied me.

All the way, I was nervous at the prospect of being back with my unit. Haaziq had told me what to tell them when I returned.

"They'll want to know where you are," I said.

"You may tell them," said Haaziq. "We will not be there. We are moving as soon as we return to camp."

"This is it," said the driver, bringing the jeep to a sudden stop.

"Your unit is that direction," said Haaziq, pointing toward the northwest. "First, though we have to do something."

He nodded to the driver, Tareet, who grabbed me in a chokehold.

"Wha . . ." I tried to say. Then I felt the crack of bone as one of the other men, Wajeeh, twisted my left arm, breaking it.

I cried out, struggling to get loose.

Tareef released me and I staggered a few feet, trying to get my balance. The pain shooting through my arm made it difficult for me to gather my senses.

But they weren't through with me yet.

When I turned to face Haaziq, he drew his gun and fired, striking me on my right side. It was like a red hot poker stabbing me. I fell to the ground.

Was this it? Had they taken me out here to kill me?

"Why?" I managed to get out.

"We are not going to kill you," said Haaziq. "But when you arrive at your base it must appear you were injured while escaping. Otherwise, they will doubt your story. It is also insurance for me and my men."

"Oh, yeah? How's that?" I asked, gritting my teeth, trying to overcome the throbbing pain in my arm and side.

"Were you not injured, you would remain with your unit. And if you have been lying to me you would turn around and resume fighting against us. I have come to like you, Quincy Bollweber, and I do not relish the prospect that either of us might kill the other.

"Since you are wounded, however, they will send you to Germany to heal and then back to America as a war hero, since you were captured and you escaped. It is there you will be of use to our cause; unless, again, you have lied to me. Now, Quincy Bollweber, it is time for you to leave. Allahu Akbar!"

"Allahu Akbar!" the other three men joined in.

"Allahu Akbar," I said . . . but with somewhat less conviction.

*****

By the time I walked from where Haaziq and his men dropped me off to where my unit was stationed I could barely stand. I was thankful the guard on duty rushed out to put an arm around me and half-carried me into the camp.

Someone called for help and within minutes I lay on a cot in a tent. The medic bent over me, cleaning my wound. He'd put a sling on my arm until he had a chance to address it.

Captain Richardson, our C.O. was also there.

"How you doing, corporal?" he asked.

"Okay, sir," I said.

"It's good to have you back and see that you're okay—relatively speaking, that is."

"Yes, sir."

"Troy'll take good care of you; then we'll have time to talk and you can fill me in on what happened to you."

I nodded. "Yes, sir."

*****

Troy must have given me something to knock me out because I didn't remember anything after that until the next morning when he woke me up.

"Let's take a look at your side," he said, removing the bandage.

It was a through and through shot, so Troy had disinfected the areas and applied bandages on both my front and back.

"Two more inches to the left," he said, "and we'd have had a serious problem."

I wondered if it were a lucky shot or if Haaziq was that good a marksman. I decided on the latter.

"How long 'til I can get out of here?" I asked.

"Tomorrow. We're shipping you to Landstuhl."

180

Haaziq was right. He was going to succeed in getting me out of Afghanistan!

"Captain's going to be by shortly. He wants to interview you."

As Troy stood to leave Captain Richardson came in.

"How's our patient today?" he asked.

"Good to go, sir," said Troy. He turned and left.

Captain Richardson pulled up a chair and sat down. "You have some explaining to do," he said.

I told the Captain how I'd ducked into a house when the firing started and then was knocked out. I told him about Haaziq and all the conversations we'd had.

"They didn't torture you?" asked the captain, a note of disbelief in his voice.

"No, sir. I guess when I was unconscious I spoke some Urdu, which made them curious about me, wondering where I'd learned it."

"How'd you make your escape?"

"I didn't escape, sir. They let me go."

For a moment the Captain didn't say anything; just stared at me.

"What do you mean, 'they let you go,'?"

"I figured the only way to escape was to pretend I was joining them, that I was converting to Islam."

"And they bought that?"

"I wasn't sure they would at first."

Truth be told, I still wasn't sure I convinced Haaziq I had crossed over.

"But apparently they did," I continued. "Afterward, I kept asking for my piece back, figuring I'd have a chance to sneak off. But Haaziq wouldn't give it to me. Finally, he told me I wouldn't be staying with him and his men, that he was sending me back here and I would serve as a spy for him."

Captain Richardson shook his head.

"And they just let you go?"

"They dropped me off a couple clicks out and I walked in. First, though, they broke my arm; then Haaziq shot me."

"Why'd they do that?"

"To make it look like I had escaped," I said.

"So this Haaziq fellow wanted you to stay here and spy for him. Not too smart of him to shoot you; now you're going to Germany, and then back home."

"Looks that way," I said.

"Okay, what can you tell me about where they are and what they have in the way of men and firepower?"

I told the Captain what I could about Haaziq and his men, how many there were, the armament they had, what their compound looked like. I told him about where I thought the camp was located.

"But they won't be there," I said.

"How do you know?"

"Haaziq told me they'd be moving as soon as they got back from dropping me off."

"We'll check it out anyway," said Captain Richardson. "Okay, you know they're going to question you further when you get to Landstuhl."

Fifteen minutes after the Captain left Shoo came rushing in.

"I just got back from patrol!" he exclaimed. "We thought you were dead!"

I smiled. "Nope, not dead—just shot and with a broken arm."

"They're sending you to Landstuhl," he said.

I nodded. "Yep. Then back home. Will you miss me?"

"You lucky bastard. You had to go get yourself captured to get out of this hell hole."

182

*****

For a fifty-year-old facility the Landstuhl Army Medical Center, located outside Landstuhl, Germany, was still a top-notch hospital, the main treatment center for wounded soldiers coming from Afghanistan.

It was considerably more comfortable than the med tent I'd come from.

Captain Richardson was right about further questioning: two days' worth from a military intelligence officer. I got the distinct feeling they didn't believe I hadn't actually converted and gone over to the other side.

Apparently, though, they eventually were convinced.

When the interrogations finished I was released and flown back to the states, to my previous post at Fort Benning, where I was assigned to light duty.

CHAPTER TWENTY-SEVEN
(twenty-one days before the Presidential election)

It had been two weeks since the discovery of Madeline James's body.

Danny and Molly were sure her death was somehow connected to the White House, specifically to the President, himself.

But where to go from there?

They couldn't very well haul him in for questioning. And repeated attempts to determine who was behind the foundation that owned the suite where Madeline lived, and made weekly deposits of money into her account—stopping, tellingly, the day her body was discovered—proved fruitless.

So they had turned their attention to the other cases on their desks, cases that held more promise of being solved.

Until the phone call came.

"Yes, this is Detective McPherson. Who did you say this was?"

"Cornel Conrad;" came the voice on the other end, "from the Oglethorpe Place?"

"Oh, yes, Mr. Conrad. I remember you. What can I do for you?"

"I remember now, seeing Miss James with someone."

"Is that right?" said Molly. "And who was it?"

"I'd rather not discuss this over the phone. Can you meet with me?"

"Sure;" said Molly, "in your office?"

"No," said Conrad. "There's a coffee shop around the corner—O'Hearn's. Can we meet there? In, say, twenty minutes?"

"We'll see you there."

"Who was that," asked Danny when Molly hung up the phone.

"The manager of The Place. He has some information for us."

"Oh, yeah? We meeting him?"

"In twenty minutes. Come on, grab your coat."

*****

Twenty minutes later Molly and Danny sat in a booth at O'Hearn's Coffee Bar. Cornel Conrad sat across from them, nervously drumming his fingers on a folded newspaper lying on the table in front of him.

"You said you remembered now that you saw Miss James with someone," said Molly.

"Yes," said Conrad. "It was several weeks before her death. I had completely forgotten about it until I saw the paper this morning. The man I saw her with—his picture is in today's paper."

"Show us," said Molly.

Conrad opened the newspaper to reveal the front page, containing a picture of Robert campaigning in Arkansas.

"That's him," said Conrad.

"The President?" said Danny, his eyebrows arching.

"No, no, the man standing next to him. Here." Conrad pointed to Jamie Inskeep. "He's the one I saw with her."

Neither Molly nor Danny could barely contain their excitement.

"That's Jamie Inskeep," said Danny.

"Where did you see them?" asked Molly.

Conrad pointed out the window to a lounge across the street. "There—at the Birmingham Bar. Sometimes I stop there after work for a drink—you know, I don't like to be seen drinking at the bar at the Oglethorpe—and they were in a back booth. I wouldn't have seen them at all except I had to pass their booth to get to the men's room."

"And you're sure this is the same man," said Danny.

"Quite sure."

"How many times have you seen them there?" asked Molly.

"Just that once."

"Okay. Mr. Conrad, you've been a great help," said Molly.

Conrad nodded, folded his paper under his arm, slid out of the booth, and left.

"We going across the street?" asked Danny.

"You bet your sweet booty we are," said Molly. "Let's pick up today's paper first, though."

*****

"No, she doesn't look familiar."

Molly and Danny had shown Madeline's picture to the bartender at the Birmingham Bar.

"She's not a regular, *that* I know," added the bartender.

Danny laid the paper on the counter. "How about this guy?" he asked, pointing to Jamie.

"Oh, Mr. Inskeep. Sure. He's here a lot. When he's in town, that is. He's the personal aide to the President, you know.

"Yes, we know," said Molly. "But you never saw him with this woman?"

The bartender shook his head. "Nope. Like I said, I don't ever remember seeing her at all."

CHAPTER TWENTY-EIGHT

Captain White wasn't sure what he had just heard.

"You want to do what?"

"We want to question Jamie Inskeep," said Molly.

She and Danny were in the captain's office, where they had shared with him the information they'd gotten from Cornel Conrad.

"Jamie Inskeep—personal aide to the President of the United States?" White shook his head.

"That's right," said Danny. "He's a person of interest."

"A person of interest. You know what kind of hornet's nest you'd be stirring up here?" asked White.

"Wouldn't be the first time," replied Molly. "Remember Watergate?"

"Not really," said White. "I wasn't even eleven when that happened."

"Yes, but you know what it was all about—and all the guys, a lot of them on Nixon's staff—who ended up in jail," said Molly. "Haldeman was Nixon's Chief of Staff."

"And Dwight Chapin was Nixon's deputy assistant, kind of like Inskeep is today," added Danny.

Captain White shrugged. "Okay, if that's what you want to do. What's your next step?"

"We'll go to his home," said Danny. "Question him there."

"Okay," said Captain White. "Go for it—but tread carefully."

*****

Molly and Danny were met in the lobby of the Meridian Square Luxury Apartments Building by a polite, but stern, attendant.

"I'm sorry;" said the man, who topped Danny by several inches and outweighed him by a good thirty pounds, "this is a private building—residents only allowed."

Danny pulled his coat back, revealing the badge on his belt. "And we'd like to speak to one of them," he said.

"Of course," said the attendant, suddenly eager to cooperate. "Which one?"

"Mr. Inskeep," said Molly.

The attendant hesitated for a moment. "Mr. Inskeep? He's—"

"We know;" said Danny, "personal aide to the President. Very muckety muck."

"Let me see if he's in," said the attendant, picking up a phone.

A few moments of conversation confirmed Jamie was, indeed, home.

"He said to send you on up," said the attendant.

*****

Smiling broadly, Jamie welcomed Molly and Danny into his apartment. They both stopped and looked around, impressed as much as P.J. had been.

189

"Some place you have here, Mr. Inskeep," said Molly, once they were all seated.

"Thank you," said Jamie. "I enjoy it."

"Does this place have a fitness center?" asked Molly. "My husband says he wants to find a place with a fitness center."

"Yes, it does," said Jamie. "But I don't use it. I usually work out in the gym at the White House."

"What's it like being personal assistant to the President?" asked Danny.

"Aide. I'm the President's personal aide. And it keeps me busy. May I ask why you're here?"

"Mr. Inskeep, I believe you know a woman named Madeline James?" said Molly.

"No, I don't believe I do," said Jamie. He smoothed his hair back with one hand. "Why, who is she?"

"She was found murdered a few weeks ago," said Danny. "And we have a witness who puts you with her at the Birmingham Bar."

For a brief moment, Jamie considered denying he ever frequented the Birmingham—then realized it was something that could be easily confirmed.

"I do frequent that establishment, but if I ever met that woman there I don't remember. And someone says they saw me with her at the Birmingham that evening? That's impossible. I was at the White House all evening—spent the night there. As you know, President Winslow's in the middle of a reelection campaign, and I had a lot of work to do."

"No, I didn't say the witness said he saw you *that* night— the night Miss James was murdered. It was several weeks earlier."

Jamie shrugged. "I wish I could help you but, honestly, I don't know the woman."

Molly handed Jamie her card. "In case anything comes to mind, give us a call, okay?"

Jamie nodded. Danny stood, followed by Molly, and the two left the apartment.

"You and Del really looking for a new place to live?" asked Danny as they rode down in the elevator.

Molly looked at him. "Are you kidding? I just wanted to see how he talked normally before we questioned him about the vic."

"And what do you think?"

"He's lying through his teeth," said Molly. "Did you hear how the tenor of his voice changed ever so slightly when we began talking about her? And how he smoothed his hair back before denying he knew her? Shit, I almost felt his nose getting longer. He didn't bother to ask how she was killed. And you know what else?"

"What's that?"

"He said he couldn't have been with her the night she was killed because he was at the White House."

"So?"

"We never told him the exact day she was killed."

"Maybe he read it in the newspaper," said Danny.

"I don't think so. When I asked if he knew her he said he didn't. Then he asked who she was."

"And?"

"If he'd read about her in the newspaper he would have known who she was—he wouldn't have asked."

*****

"What do you mean *they were at your apartment?*"

Robert glared down at a very uncomfortable Jamie, who had just told him about the two detectives' visit.

"They were asking questions about Madeline."

"What kind of questions?"

"Someone said they saw me with her in a bar."

Robert's eyes widened. "And did they? Did someone see you with her in a bar?"

For the second time that day, Jamie considered lying, as he had thought about doing to the detectives about going to the Birmingham. But he knew Robert would see right through him. Better to be honest.

"One time. She thought she should have a Secret Service agent assigned to her."

"A *what?*"

"A Secret Service agent. She said Mrs. Winslow has Secret Service agents and she thought she should, too."

"That crazy fucked-up bitch!" Robert erupted. "It's a damn good thing she *is* dead."

"She insisted on meeting with me in person. I knew we couldn't do it at her place or here in the White House, so we met in a bar I stop at occasionally."

"And what did you tell her?" asked Robert.

"I told her she was out of her fucking mind. There was no way she was getting a Secret Service agent. The whole idea was to keep her out of sight, not draw attention to her."

"And what did she say?"

"She wasn't happy, but I gave her some perks to shut her up."

Robert sighed. "Okay, so she's shut up for good now. And whatever's going on with this investigation into her death, I want it shut down."

"You want me to take care of it like I took care of Madeline?"

Robert looked at Jamie incredulously and shook his head. "I'll ask you the same thing you told Madeline—are you out of your fucking mind? We're talking about police officers, here. We don't kill police officers. That only makes matters worse. I'm sure you can find some other way, lower profile, to make sure this investigation gets killed."

"Yes, sir, I'm sure I can."

CHAPTER TWENTY-NINE
(nineteen days until the Presidential election)

Robert, along with a dozen members of his administration, among them five high-ranking military officials, sat around the conference table in the situation room, listening to a report from General William Weatherford on the war in Guinea.

"We pretty much have the rebels pushed back into two areas: the northwest corner, including Boké and in the south where they still hold Nzérékoréo."

"What's the holdup, Willie," asked Robert. "Why aren't we getting them out of those two areas?"

"They're getting a lot of support from Mauritania," replied General Weatherford.

"And Burkina Faso," spoke up General Baumgardner. "President Oumaru is sending guns, ammunition, and supplies to them."

"Oumaru?" said Robert. "Where the hell is he getting money to be supplying anything to anybody? Burkina Faso's the poorest country on the whole fucking continent!"

"Egypt," said Baumgardner.

Robert's face turned three shades of red. His fists clenched. "Egypt? Fucking Egypt?"

As Robert was speaking a Marine Corporal entered the room and stopped behind him.

"I want it stopped!" shouted Robert. "I don't give a shit what we have to do, I want it stopped! And I want it stopped now!"

The Corporal reached down and laid a note in front of Robert.

Robert picked it up and read it to himself.

"Yes, sir," said Admiral Sato. "What we have—"

"Excuse me," said Robert. "Something's come up. We'll have to cut this short. Admiral Sato, I want a full report on my desk by tomorrow morning."

*****

Robert found a distraught Lilly Adkins in the hallway outside the Situation Room wringing her hands.

"Where is she?" asked Robert.

"In the Vermeil Room. I tried to—"

Robert waved her off. "I'll handle it."

He entered the Vermeil Room and shut the door behind him.

Portraits of seven former first ladies—Eleanor Roosevelt, Lady Bird Johnson, Jacqueline Kennedy, Nancy Reagan, Pat Nixon, Lou Hoover, and Michelle Obama—hung on the walls.

Sprawled out in a Rococo Revival needlepoint armchair and obviously drunk, Wilma held a nearly empty gin bottle. Tears streamed down her face.

Robert went over and squatted down in front of his wife.

"What's going on?" he asked, gently.

Still sobbing, Wilma said, "Look at all those beautiful women." She waved her hand, indicating the portraits. "I'll never have my picture up there."

Robert took the gin bottle from her hand and placed it on the floor. Then he took both of her hands in his.

"Yes, you will, dear."

"No, no I won't," said Wilma. "Look at them! They're beautiful and elegant. I'm old. And I'm ugly. And I'm a drunken slob. I'm a mess."

"Mother, I promise you . . . you will have your portrait up there." Robert pointed to Michelle Obama's portrait. "See that space right there, the one where the nigger is? That's where we'll hang your portrait."

"But what about Mrs. Obama?"

"I promise. We'll find a more appropriate place for her picture. In fact," he added, smiling, "if you want, I'll call a portrait artist right now and have him come in this evening to paint you."

Wilma laughed. "Because I look so damn good, right?"

"Come on," said Robert, getting to his feet. "Let's get you to your room."

Wilma tried to stand but began to stagger.

"I don't think I can."

"I'll help you." Robert picked her up, walked over to the closed door, and kicked it.

The same Marine Corporal who brought him the note quickly opened the door.

"Sir, do you need—?"

"I'm fine, corporal, thank you."

The Marine watched as Robert carried Wilma down the corridor.

*****

Lilly hovered nearby as Robert pulled the covers up to Wilma's neck.

"Mr. President, do you want me to—?"

"Thank you, Lilly. You can leave now. I'll stay with her tonight."

CHAPTER THIRTY
(eighteen days until the presidential election)

Wendy leaned back in her chair and stared at the computer in front of her. It had been a long day. She glanced out the window—nothing but darkness.

"I gotta get a life," she mumbled to herself.

She heard a stirring in the other room.

Who . . .? she wondered.

The door opened.

"Hey, how's it going?" asked Lisa, standing in the doorway.

Wendy was surprised—and pleased—to see her.

"Money's still coming in," said Wendy. "The way you're spending it, we can't afford to let up."

"I'm doing my best. Anybody else here tonight?" asked Lisa.

Wendy shook her head. "You and me and the mice—that's it. I have something to show you. Come on."

She stood and moved toward the back door.

Lisa followed and found herself in a room filled with filing cabinets and a sofa in one corner. Wendy closed the door and locked it. The two embraced and kissed, hard and deep.

Lisa leaned her head back and looked at Wendy. "You know, if dickhead ever found out about us, he'd have us canned."

"Shit, we're lucky we don't have balls, or he'd have us castrated."

They both laughed, continuing to hold one another.

"I've missed you," said Wendy.

"Yeah, you get to work here in this office while I have to traipse around the country with Bobo."

"You know it's not nice to refer to your president like that."

"I thought I *was* being nice. I *could* have called him a lot worse. And get this—the bastard tried to hit on me?"

"You're shitting me!"

Lisa shook her head. "No way. We were in Philadelphia. He had me come to his hotel room, said he wanted to talk about some strategy. The only strategy he had in mind was how to get me into bed."

"What did you do?" asked Wendy.

She let go of Lisa. They walked over and sat down on the sofa.

"I told him as intriguing as that sounded, I didn't see how I could possibly continue on the campaign if we were sleeping together. He said he wasn't looking for a relationship, just a quick roll in the hay."

"He said that?"

"Yeah, a quick roll in the hay. I said no, I felt if we did it once I'd want to do it again, and if that happened I'd have to quit. So he backed off, said he didn't want to lose me; told me to forget the whole thing."

"And that was it?"

"Except for the five hundred bucks a week raise he gave me to keep quiet."

"No way! You devil, you!"

"I told my sister about it. She asked me how I can work for the dumb ass, knowing how I feel about him."

"What did you say?"

"My sister's a defense lawyer. I told her it was a job, that's all. A job that pays damned good."

"Even better now."

"Yeah," said Lisa. "I said it's no different than when she represents one of her slimeball clients. Why do you work for him, Wendy?"

"Same reason—I need the money. But enough about him. Now take your clothes off."

"And why should I do that?"

"Because I want a quick roll in the hay."

CHAPTER THIRTY-ONE
(fifteen days until the Presidential election)

Molly no sooner took off her coat and hung it up than Oren Adams, another detective in the unit, called out to her.

"Hey, Molly, the captain says he wants to see you asap."

"Christ," Molly muttered under her breath. *I bet he wants to know where we are on the James murder.*

Minutes later she was standing in the captain's office.

"Captain, you wanted to see me," said Molly,

"Sit down. I have some papers for you to sign."

"Papers?" said Molly.

Captain White pushed the papers across the desk to her.

Molly sat down and quickly skimmed them.

"These are retirement papers. I'm not retiring."

"Yeah, you are;" said White, "effective immediately."

"Is this a joke?"

"No joke—the word came down from upstairs: you're to take immediate retirement."

"But . . . but, why? I don't want to retire. I can't *afford* to retire."

"Sure you can. You're going to get full retirement benefits, plus—"

"Full? But that's less than what I'm making now. And I can't even live on that. I got two boys—"

199

"Full benefits plus a new consulting job that will pay you *more* than you're earning from the city."

Molly leaned back in her chair.

"A job? This is crazy! I haven't applied for any job."

"You'll be working as a security specialist for a large firm out in Silver Springs; that, plus your retirement? You won't have any trouble paying for your kids' education now and getting caught up on your house payments."

"How . . . how do you know about all this?" asked Molly.

"Doesn't matter. What does matter is I need your piece and your badge. I'll need you to have your desk cleared out by noon. And you start your new job on Monday. They'll contact you in the next few days."

Molly's brain spun, trying to take in what was happening: retirement? A new job? It didn't make sense. Then she thought about the money.

"How much more?" she asked.

"How much more what?"

"How much more will I be making than what I'm making now?"

"I don't know. What difference does it make? That along with your retirement—you'll be sitting in hog heaven."

"Can I ask why? Why this is happening?"

Captain White shook his head. "I haven't the faintest idea. I'm only following orders. Tell you the truth, I hate to see you go—you're a pretty good detective. But this is a great opportunity for you. Your retirement party's planned for Friday. Anything else?"

Molly thought for a moment. What else could there be? She was retiring. She was going to have a new job. She'd be making more money. She shrugged.

*****

Thirty minutes later Danny walked into the squad room.

"Where's Molly?" he asked of no one in particular.

"Gone," said one of the other detectives.

"Gone? Gone where?"

"Home, I suppose. She retired—left the force."

Danny stared at the detective, unable to speak.

Minutes later he was in Captain White's office. "Molly's gone?" he said.

"Retired," said White. "It was time."

"I don't believe it! She never said nothing to me."

"It was kind of sudden. One more thing;" added Captain White, "you've been transferred to the liaison squad that works with Homeland Security. No change in your rank, but a nice bump in pay."

For the second time in less than fifteen minutes, Danny was speechless.

"Starting when?" he asked, finally.

"Immediately. You're to report today. Now, we're having a retirement party for Molly here Friday. I expect you'll want to come back for it."

"What about all the cases we're working? Who's going to take those over?"

"I'll reassign them. In fact, why don't you bring all the files in to me now, before you leave?"

A few minutes later Danny returned and laid a stack of folders on the captain's desk.

Captain White reached up and shook Danny's hand. "It's been great working with you, Danny. Good luck in your new assignment."

Still in shock, Danny nodded, mumbled a 'thanks,' then turned and walked out of the office.

Captain White sat down and leafed through the files Danny brought him. He stopped when he came to the one for which he was searching: Madeline James.

One by one, he removed the papers from the folder and ran them through the shredder next to his desk. When he finished, he took the manila folder they had been in and ran it through.

Then he sorted the remaining files into three separate stacks.

*****

Molly's family was thrilled with the news.

"You're quitting the force?" asked Kiki. "For real?"

"Retiring—with full benefits."

"And you have another job already?" asked Del.

Molly nodded. "Start Monday."

"Looks like our money problems are solved," said Del. A big grin spread across his face.

"Looks like," said Molly.

Ryan hurried to answer the ring of the phone. "Mom, it's for you," he said, handing it to her.

"Hey, I hear you're retiring," came Danny's voice from the other end of the line.

"Yep; came as a big surprise to me. I had to be gone by noon and you weren't in yet so I couldn't say goodbye."

"I've got a surprise myself," said Danny. "I got a promotion."

"A promotion?"

"Yep. I've been transferred to the liaison squad that works with Homeland Security; won't be working Homicide anymore."

"So, who's going to be working our cases now?"

"I don't know. The captain said to bring him all our files, so I did."

"Including Madeline James's file?"

"Yep, everything."

"Interesting," said Molly.

"What is?" asked Danny.

"Both of us leaving at the same time."

Molly had a feeling the investigation into the death of Madeline James was, for all intents and purposes, finished.

CHAPTER THIRTY- TWO

Mrs. Carlisle fluffed Alice's pillow and adjusted the spread that covered her.

Alice didn't move. Her eyes were closed, her breathing labored in spite of the nasal cannula she wore.

Mrs. Carlisle had tried to get a little soup down her, but Alice turned it away.

When the doorbell rang, Mrs. Carlisle hurried to answer it.

"Oh, I'm so glad you're here," she said, opening the door to let P.J. in.

"I came as soon as I could. She's worse?"

"She's having a lot of trouble breathing. The doctor just left. He said there wasn't much more he could do. Where's Muhammad?"

"He and the band left last night for a gig in upstate New York. He'll be back in a week."

Mrs. Carlisle shook her head. "You better call him and tell him to come back now. I don't think she has a week."

P.J. nodded, took out her cell phone, and punched in numbers as she followed Mrs. Carlisle down the hallway.

"Yeah, as soon as you can," said P.J., as she entered Alice's room. She closed the phone and slid it into her pocket.

"Hey," said P.J. going over to the bed.

Alice opened her eyes.

P.J. took her hand.

"Hey, Sweetie. How you doing?" asked Alice, with some difficulty.

"I'm doing fine. How you feeling?"

"Hanging in there;" said Alice, a raspiness in her voice, "just . . . hanging in there. You know—one day at a time."

"Muhammad's out of town, but he'll be back this evening."

"That's nice. Can you stay awhile?"

P.J. sat down on the bed next to Alice. "You bet. I got nothing else on my schedule. You want to watch some T.V.?"

"Will you read to me?"

"Sure. What would you like to hear?"

Alice gestured with her hand. "My Bible's over there on the shelf; anything from it."

P.J. walked over to the shelf, found the Bible, returned to the bed, and sat down. She opened the book and checked the Table of Contents in the front, then turned to the Psalms and found the passage for which she was looking.

She began to read. "The Lord is my shepherd . . ."

*****

P.J. paced the floor of the kitchen, alternately taking drags off her cigarette and swigs of beer from the bottle in her hand.

"Why don't you sit down?" asked Muhammad, seated at the table, a can of soda in front of him.

"I don't know what to do. I'm not sure what to do with what I have."

"Have you told your boss what you found out?"

"Not yet." P.J. stopped her pacing long enough to throw the empty bottle into a trash can and retrieve another from the refrigerator. "I want to get a little more before I do."

205

"How you going to do that?"

P.J. stopped and stared out the window. "I have an idea if Clancy will go along with it."

*****

John Clancy didn't much care for P.J.'s idea.

"Why can't Harry ask your question—whatever it is?" he asked. "Plus, he's much more likely to be called on than you are."

P.J. had broached the possibility of Clancy letting her attend the President's next White House Press Briefing.

"I want to see the reaction on his face. I want to see if he'll deny it or what."

"I think I should know what the fucking question is, don't you?" asked Clancy.

"Don't you trust me?"

"Shit no. For all I know you're going to accuse him of fucking some prostitute."

"Hell, even you know he's doing that: you told me so. But that's not what I'm after."

"And you won't tell me?"

"I'm serious. Trust me on this one. This could be big."

Clancy threw up his hands in defeat. "Okay. I'll tell Harry to sit this one out."

P.J. jumped up, ran around the desk, and threw her arms around Clancy.

"Oh, thank you, thank you, thank you so much, Daddykins!"

"Get the fuck out of here," growled Clancy, faking a scowl.

CHAPTER THIRTY-THREE
(thirteen days until the Presidential election)

In spite of living in and around the District her whole life, P.J. had never been in the White House.

She tried her best to hide the nervousness she felt as she waited in line at the Southeast Gate, clutching the press pass Clancy had obtained for her.

She had chosen a silk dress from her closet she thought might be sexy enough to get Winslow's attention, but not so suggestive that she looked like a floozy; certainly nothing like what she'd worn when she managed to hook up with Jamie.

After the guard waved her through, she quickly made her way to the West Wing where the James S. Brady Press Briefing Room was located. Harry had given her thorough instructions on where to go and how to act. The former she followed to a "T." She wasn't sure about the latter.

Her first thought when she entered the room was how small it was. It always appeared much larger when she'd seen it on television. But, not much more expansive than a slightly larger living room, the back section was crammed with high-tech television cameras and other recording equipment.

Forty-eight seats—six across and eight deep—accommodated the correspondents who had come to attend the latest briefing. Representing the Eagle, P.J. was fortunate to be assigned a place at the end of the front row.

While she waited with the other reporters for the President to appear, she struck up a conversation with Lindsey Peabody, longtime White House Correspondent for the New York Daily Press, who was sitting next to her.

"Haven't met you before," said Lindsey. "First time here?"

"First time in the White House."

"Oh? What happened to Harry?"

"Had a doctor's appointment—couldn't break it."

"Well, welcome to the zoo."

"I guess Brady was quite a man, wasn't he?" said P.J. "To have this room named after him."

"Yes, he was. I knew him."

"You did?" exclaimed P.J., impressed.

"I was a cub reporter back in 1981 when he was the White House Press Secretary. And I was outside the Hilton the day he and Reagan were shot. It was a madhouse."

"Wow. So you were an eyewitness."

"I was; made quite a story."

"What did I hear about a pool here?" asked P.J.

"You're sitting on it."

"Huh?"

"The pool was installed back in the thirties for Roosevelt to use. He had polio, you know."

P.J. nodded.

"When Nixon was in office he had the pool drained and this room built over it for use by the press. At one time there was a trap door up by the podium that led down to where the pool used to be. Back in '07 a stairwell was built behind the podium in place of the trapdoor."

"Fascinating. Listen, can you give me some tips—fill me in on how this works?"

"The press conference?"

"Yeah, I don't want to look like a doofus."

For the next several minutes Lindsey schooled P.J. on how the conference worked, who got to ask questions, and what the protocol was.

He'd barely finished when Winslow entered with his entourage, including Jamie.

"The President of the United States," intoned Marcus Sharp, the Press Secretary.

Everyone rose to their feet.

"Please be seated," said Robert when he reached the podium. His eyes went directly to P.J., then around the room. "I'll be happy to take your questions now."

Hands shot up.

"Mr. Toppler," said Robert.

Andy Toppler of USA TV stood. "Sir, it seems there's been some difficulty in getting information about how the war in Guinea is progressing. Can you fill us in?"

"Much of the information is highly classified," said Robert. "I can tell you our troops have the situation in hand, and that total victory is in the near future."

Everyone applauded. Hands shot up again, including P.J.'s.

Winslow ignored her and continued to call on other reporters whom he recognized. Twenty minutes later, he turned to P.J., who by now was frantically waving her hand.

"Uh, yes? I'm sorry, I don't know your name."

P.J. stood up. "P.J. Landreth, sir, with the Washington Eagle."

Jamie's eyes widened and his jaw dropped open.

"You're here in place of Mr. Anderson."

"Yes, sir. Mr. President, I wonder what you can tell us about Operation Crusade?"

Robert's face hardened, and his jaws clenched. For a moment he hesitated, then said, "Operation Crusade? I'm sorry, Miss . . . ?"

"Landreth, sir. With the Washington Eagle."

Robert straightened to his full height. "Yes, Miss Landreth, I'm sorry but I don't know anything about any Operation Crusade."

"But, sir—"

Robert looked away to another reporter. Though she didn't have her hand up, Robert called on her. "Miss Kincaid."

P.J. started to speak again. "But, sir—"

Robert looked back at P.J., his eyes narrowed. "Miss Landreth, I've called on Miss Kincaid. Please take your seat."

P.J. remained standing for a few moments before Lindsey gently took her by her arm and eased her into her seat.

"Don't push it," he whispered.

As the conference continued, Robert several times glanced P.J.'s way. From the look on his face it was apparent he was upset.

Following the last question—at least the last one Robert felt like answering—the White House group exited, followed by the press correspondents.

Jamie waited for P.J. outside the room. When she emerged, he grabbed her arm and hustled her down the hall into the Palm Room, which was empty at the time, and pushed her up against a wall.

"What the fuck's going on?" he asked, angrily. "Who are you?"

"You should be more careful who you sleep with."

"You bitch! You drugged my drink, didn't you? And you went snooping in my briefcase. That's how you know about Operation Crusade."

P.J. faked a look of surprise. "Operation Crusade? Why, your boss said he didn't know anything about any Operation Crusade. Is this some little operation of your own you're keeping from him?"

Furious, Jamie pointed his finger at P.J. "Listen, you—"

Just then Lindsey came through the door.

"P.J., there you are. Some of us are going for a drink. I thought you might want to join us."

"I'd love to," said P.J., freeing herself from Jamie's grasp.

She slipped her arm through Lindsey's and led him from the room, leaving Jamie standing alone, still seething with anger.

*****

Robert paced the floor of the Oval Office, a combination of agitation and anger propelling him. Jamie and Nate sat silently on the couch nearby.

"Okay," said Robert, "I want to know how the fuck that woman found out about Operation Crusade, and how much she knows." He stared hard at the two men. "Either of you happen to know?"

"Sir, I have no idea," said Nate. "I don't even know who she is. But I'll get right on it."

Robert's gaze shifted to Jamie. "Jamie?"

For an instant, Jamie considered telling the truth, as he had when he'd been asked by the two detectives about frequenting the Birmingham. This time he decided lying was his better option.

"No, sir. But I'll see what I can find out."

"I don't want this to go any farther, understood?" said Robert.

"Yes, sir," both men replied.

"Nate, give me a minute with Jamie."

Nate got up and left the room.

Robert stared at Jamie. "I don't know if you're involved in this or not, but when I say I don't want it to go any farther, I mean *any* farther."

"You want me to take care of it like I did Madeline?"

Robert thought for a moment. "Not unless it's absolutely necessary. But before you do anything, make sure the damn recording of this conversation gets lost."

*****

P.J. was on page 245 of Woodward and Bernstein's book, *All The President's Men*, engrossed in reading about Woodward's meeting in a parking garage with "Deep Throat"—later identified as former FBI official Mark Felt—as the latter confirmed the involvement of Attorney General John Mitchell and Charles Colson, Special Counsel to President Nixon in the break-in at the Democratic National Headquarters at the Watergate complex.

The jangling of her cell phone startled her. Reluctantly, she placed a marker between the pages and laid the book down.

"Hey, Sweetie," she said, thinking it was Muhammad, who said he'd call.

"Hello, Miss Landreth," came the reply from a voice that sounded familiar.

P.J. instantly became more alert. "Who is this?" she asked.

"This is your boyfriend—you know, the one you drugged and then fucked when you went through my briefcase. And I didn't even enjoy getting fucked."

"How did you get my private number? What do you want?"

212

Jamie's sneering laugh came through the phone. "I'm the President's personal aide. I can get anybody's fucking phone number I want. And what do I want? I want you to forget everything you read about Operation Crusade. I want you to destroy any notes you might have about it and anything on your computer. I want the whole topic obliterated from your life."

"Gee," said P.J., sarcastically, "that's a lot to ask. And why should I do all of that?"

"Because pursuing this matter any further could definitely be hazardous to your health."

"Are you threatening me?" asked P.J., now not feeling as calm as she had a few seconds earlier.

"Wow," said Jamie, "you're not as stupid as I thought. Yes, you're goddamn right—I'm *threatening* you!"

"Although it seems to me I'm the one who could be threatening you," said P.J. "What do you suppose your boss— that would be President Winslow, right?—what do you suppose he would do if he found out how I got my information?"

Jamie was furious. "You little bitch! You have no idea what you're getting yourself into. Do you know what I could do to you? You say anything to the President—or anybody— and . . . well, trust me, you don't want to know."

"This conversation is over," said P.J. "Don't call me again. Oh—and I think you're going to find some interesting reading in Sunday's paper . . . front page. Don't miss it."

P.J. closed her phone. Her hand shook.

On the other end, Jamie was livid. "Don't say I didn't warn you," he said to the now silent phone in his hand.

CHAPTER THIRTY-FOUR
(twelve days until the Presidential election)

"Whatta you got for me?" asked Clancy.

P.J. had been summoned to Clancy's office as soon as she walked into the newsroom.

"You said you were on to something. When am I going to get this big story you been working on?"

"I'm meeting someone when I leave here. He's agreed to give me more information."

"Who's that?"

"My uncle. The same guy who put me on to this in the first place."

"Your uncle?"

"Let's call him my uncle. I should have the story on your desk tomorrow morning for Sunday's edition."

"This had better be one hell of a story. Now, get out of here." Clancy waved his hand.

"It's going to win us a Pulitzer," said P.J. as she closed the door behind her.

She glanced at her watch as she exited the building onto Thirteenth Street. She was scheduled to meet Uncle Willie in an hour and a half. He had promised to give her more information on Operation Crusade.

214

She turned down an alley—a shortcut to her car, parked some distance away on another street.

"And I better get a goddamn parking space out of this, too," she mumbled. "I'm tired of walking three fucking blocks to my car."

Suddenly she stopped. Had she heard footsteps? She looked around but saw nothing. *Just nerves*, she thought. She picked up her pace.

More footsteps.

She glanced back again and saw what she thought was a shadow. Was it? She continued walking, this time faster, almost at a trot. Her foot hit a loose brick and she tumbled forward onto her knees, barely catching herself before smashing to the ground.

She felt a hand on her arm.

"You okay, lady?"

P.J. looked up into the eyes of a man: dirty, smelly—probably homeless. Afraid, she tried to scream, but nothing came out.

"Don't be skeered," the man said, helping her to her feet. "I ain't goin' to hurt you. Looks like you can take care of that part yourself."

P.J. looked down at her knee, blood lazily coursing from a cut.

"Th . . . thank you," she managed.

"No problem. You be more careful, now."

He turned and disappeared down the alley in the direction from which she had just come.

She retrieved her briefcase, hurried on, and in a few minutes reached the safety of her car. She quickly unlocked the door, jumped in, pulled the door shut, pushed down the lock, and gave a sigh of relief.

Still shaking, she took her cell phone from her briefcase and punched in Muhammad's number. After he'd returned from New York following P.J.'s call, he'd hooked up with a local band playing at a small club in the Georgetown neighborhood.

She was happy when his voice came through on the other end.

"Hello?"

"Oh, Honey," said P.J., still trying to catch her breath. "I'm glad I got you."

"You caught me on a five-minute break from rehearsal. You okay? You don't sound right."

"Jesus, I don't know. You know, I'm working on this story, but I'm beginning to get a little paranoid. I got a phone call—a sort of a warning phone call—from somebody high up in the administration. I mean, *really* high up."

With her free hand, P.J. pulled out a pack of cigarettes, removed one, and lit it.

"And just now I had a feeling someone was following me. I fell down—"

"You okay?"

"Yeah, yeah, I'm okay. Right now I'm on my way to a meeting with Uncle Willie. I'll come home when I'm done."

P.J. put the key in the ignition and turned it.

At that moment the drummer belted out a paradiddle. Muhammad put one hand over his ear to better hear.

"Yeah, sure that's—"

The sound of an explosion erupting through the phone almost drove him back up against the wall.

"P.J.! P.J.!" Muhammad cried out frantically. "P.J.!"

There was no response.

*****

216

A fireball lit up the night sky, revealing the blown-out windows of the building next to P.J.'s car, now a fiery mass of melting metal. Within minutes, the sound of sirens filled the air, followed by the screeching of tires as two police cars and a fire engine descended on the scene.

Firefighters quickly hooked up a hose to the nearest fireplug and proceeded to extinguish the blaze, while a knot of onlookers watched nearby.

"How many?" the Fire Chief asked one of his men.

"Far as we can tell, there was only one person in the car. No way to know right now if it was a man or woman."

The Fire Chief nodded. "We'll let the M.E. figure it. She's on her way now."

CHAPTER THIRTY-FIVE
(eleven days until the Presidential election)

Muhammad sat with his face in his hands. He couldn't believe what the two detectives sitting across the room had told him, that P.J. had been killed in an explosion.

He'd made frantic phone calls to Alice's home and as many of P.J.'s friends for whom he had numbers. No one knew anything. He'd called the newspaper office, where John Clancy, her editor, confirmed she'd left shortly before Muhammad talked with her, but he had no idea where she'd gone or where she might be. Their conversation had been a quick one; Clancy said something had happened close by, and he needed to get a reporter to the scene. Before Muhammad could ask what it was, Clancy had hung up.

Dozens of calls to hospitals and the police proved equally fruitless. Not knowing where else to turn, he'd left the club and gone home to wait, sitting up the whole night anticipating—and hoping for—P.J.'s return.

Instead, it was two detectives who arrived in the morning. They'd been able to determine the address from the license plate on what was left of P.J.'s car.

Now they sat, asking questions.

"Did Miss Landreth have any enemies you know of?" asked one of the officers.

218

"I can't think of anyone who would hurt her. Everybody loved her."

"I have to ask;" said the second detective, "where were you last night about ten-thirty?"

"At the Emerald Bar. I was sitting in with a country-western band. My own band's still in Clarence—New York. We started around nine. I left about eleven."

"You left? Was your gig over? After two hours?" asked the first detective.

"No, we were scheduled to go until two. But I was on the phone with P.J. when I heard a loud bang, and the phone went dead. I spent the next half hour calling around, trying to find her, but I couldn't. I even called the police, but they didn't have any information. So I came home and waited for her to show up."

"I'm sure plenty of people can verify you were at the bar?"

"Yeah, about two hundred. You know, you asked about enemies—P.J. was working on a story; a big one, I think."

"A story?"

"For the newspaper. She's . . . she was a reporter."

"Do you know what the story was about?" asked the second detective.

"Operation Crusade."

"Operation Crusade? What's that?"

Muhammad jumped up and began to pace. "It had something to do with the White House. That's all I know. She said it was going to be the biggest story of her career. You might check with her editor, Mr. Clancy."

"We'll do that," said the second detective. "We'll let you know what we find out."

*****

219

"Nice digs."

Molly looked up from her desk to find Danny standing in the doorway of her office.

"Hey, Danny, come on in."

Once inside, Danny looked around the room, sparsely but immaculately furnished. Pictures of Molly's three children hung on the wall; another, of Del, sat on her desk.

"It's not much, but it sure beats the District," said Molly, waving Danny to sit down.

"Sure does," Danny agreed.

"What brings you by? Wanted to see how the other side lives?"

"Crap, you always did live better than me. So, how's the job going?"

"Can't complain; home every night by five or six—every weekend off. I'm starting to know my kids better now—which may or may not be a good thing. And how's Homeland Security? You keeping us all safe?"

Danny shrugged. "Got to admit, what I'm doing's a lot tamer than being out on the streets, hunting the bad guys. But it's okay. Say, you remember Scotty McCallister?"

Molly's eyes furrowed, as she dug through her memory. "Oh, yeah, the new kid who came in around the first of the month, right before you and I got the heave-ho."

"Heave-ho. Yeah, that's a good one. Anyway, Scottie called me up yesterday, wanted to know about the Madeline James case."

Molly's eyes lit up. "He did?"

"Yeah. Says him and his partner caught a car bombing last night that might have a White House connection. Said he remembered we thought there was one with the James case."

"What'd you tell him?"

"I told him everything we knew about it. Suggested he pull the case file and check it out."

"And did he?"

"That's the strange part. Says he looked for it, but it seems to have disappeared. Says he asked Captain White about it and was told it was being handled. When Scottie mentioned the possibility of the two cases being connected—with the White House stuff and all—he says the Captain blew him off, shuffled him out of his office."

Molly leaned back in her chair, laced her fingers together, and laid them on her stomach.

"Somebody's covering up something," she said.

"That's what I figure, too," said Danny.

"But you know what?" asked Molly.

"What?"

Molly shook her head. "Not my problem. Not yours either, now."

Danny sat silent for a few moments. "Somebody should do something," he said, finally.

"Yeah," said Molly. "Somebody sure should . . . but not us."

QUINCY'S STORY - CHAPTER X

I'd been back at Fort Benning about two months when Captain Jepperson, my commanding officer, approached me and asked me to consider an early reenlistment.

"Actually, sir," I said, "I've been thinking about something else."

"Oh? What's that?"

"I've been studying up on this Green to Gold program the Army has, and I'm kind of interested in it."

"You want to become an officer?"

"I'm sure it pays better . . . doesn't it, sir?"

"It does—by a damn sight. What field are you interested in?"

"I took a few computer science classes in high school and I liked them. I think that's the direction I'd want to go."

"That would be a good career choice, whether you intended to stay in or not."

"Oh, I do," I said. "I'm in it for the long run."

"Okay, then," said the Captain. "I'll see what I can do to get you started. You have a school in mind?"

"I'm thinking of Detroit Tech."

"Why there?"

"In addition to the computer science, they also offer Arabic. I know some Urdu and picked up some Arabic while I was in Afghanistan. I think I'd like to become more fluent in it."

"Okay," said the Captain. "I'll see that you get the paperwork you need to apply. I think you'd make a great candidate and a fine officer."

*****

As much as 1999 was the worst year of my life, my four years at Detroit Technical University were some of the best.

I'd been an okay student in high school and, although college work was a lot harder, I found it stimulating. My first year was dedicated to ensuring I got off to a good start, academically. The ROTC classes were pretty much a breeze compared to what I'd undergone in basic training and being on the ground in Afghanistan.

My second year I reconnected with Shoo, who had finished up his enlistment and gotten out. He had moved back to Dearborn. It wasn't far from where I went to school so I spent a lot of my free time at his home and got to know many of his friends, almost all of whom were Muslim.

I was also put into contact with Sa'ood, who was to be my contact with the Taliban for the next five years.

I met regularly—separately, of course—with both him and Captain McCleod, my Army contact for intelligence, although neither expected me to provide much useful information to them while I was in school.

I dated somewhat, but nothing serious ever came from it. I had pretty much decided I probably would never find anyone I wanted to marry. Memona was still on my mind and in my heart.

So I put in my four years at Tech, did okay with my studies and ROTC. I'd been assured once I graduated and was commissioned a Second Lieutenant I would return to active duty, something I looked forward to with renewed enthusiasm.

CHAPTER THIRTY- SIX
(eight days until the Presidential election)

Robert had had a fit—"raised a stink," as Wilma put it—when he found out she'd paid seven thousand dollars for a chair. That was almost four years ago, shortly before they moved into the White House.

The outgoing president and his wife were taking all their furniture with them. Wilma couldn't bear the thought of moving into their new home—into the White House!—with the furnishings Robert had insisted on for the governor's mansion in Austin.

"It's all tacky;" she'd said, "vulgar."

"It's Texas," he'd disagreed.

"My point, exactly," said Wilma. "It's all 'cowboy' stuff. We're moving into the most visible home in the nation, in the *world*. We should look as though we have some taste—something other than 'wild west'."

They'd struck a bargain: she allowed him to bring a few of the less obnoxious items, but for the most part, they bought everything else new.

The chair, however, was a shock.

"Seven thousand dollars?" he'd exploded. "What the hell? We furnished our whole house for less than that when we got married. Send it back—I'm not paying seven thousand dollars for a fucking chair."

"First of all," countered Wilma, "it's not a 'fucking' chair. And secondly, you're not paying for it—it's coming out of my money. *My* money. And it's *my* chair."

When the chair arrived, Robert had to admit it was a beauty: something, he acknowledged—to himself, but not Wilma—he would have loved to have had in the governor's mansion back in Texas.

A Metropole Club Chair with large, rounded arms, and a tall back, it was finished in distressed leather which gave it a warm, rich feeling. The arms and back were set off with hand-applied nail trims.

Wilma let Robert sit in it—once. Then she announced it was going into her dressing room.

That was where Robert found her when he went looking for her: curled up in her chair in front of the window staring out onto the northeast courtyard, a scotch in her hand.

"Try not to get too sloshed," he said, making no attempt to hide his disapproval. "You know the debate is this evening."

"You know what the worst part is," she asked, not looking up.

"The worst part of what?"

"Our marriage."

"No, Wilma," said Robert, a tone of disgust in his voice. "Tell me what the worst part of our marriage is, other than your drinking."

"The fact that you despise me. You have no respect for me."

"No, that's not—"

"Oh, shut up!" barked Wilma. She turned her head and glared at him. "Just shut up! I know it and you know it. And it's not only how you treat me when we're together. I know about all your whoring around—the interns, and the reporters. And the prostitutes. By the way, whatever happened to Madeline?"

"You're drunk," said Robert, reaching for her glass.

She held it away at arm's length, just out of his reach.

"I know you only married me for my money—my family's money. And it paid off for you, didn't it? Look where you are now—the fucking President of the fucking United States." She spat the words out as if they were a bitter piece of food.

"I think it's better if you don't come tonight," said Robert.

"Oh, I'm coming. I'm coming all right."

She looked up at him.

"I'll tell you this, though. If you should win this election, I'll stay with you for another four years and that's it. If you don't win next Tuesday, I'm filing for divorce on Wednesday."

Before Robert could answer, Wilma jumped up and stormed from the room, leaving a bewildered husband behind.

CHAPTER THIRTY-SEVEN

A buzz of conversation filled the packed auditorium. TV cameras were positioned throughout the room. Two large screens flanked a stage that contained matching podiums, an empty chair, and a table on which a microphone and a folder rested.

Ellis Evans and Greg Holcomb, announcers for WBC, one of the networks telecasting the debate, sat off to one side.

"Folks," said Ellis, "here we are at the George H. W. Bush Convention Center in Washington, D.C., the site of the one and only presidential debate."

"And what a beautiful facility it is;" added Greg, "less than a year old."

"Greg, five weeks ago we were expecting this debate to be between the President and Senator Gerald McClaren."

"That's right, Ellis. But the senator's untimely passing changed all that. Now we're anticipating what shapes up to be a showdown between President Winslow and his Democratic opponent, Governor Bobby Winslow of California."

"Who is also the President's son," said Ellis, "as well as the first openly gay candidate ever to be nominated to run for president."

"And who was a relative unknown outside of California until this past August when he gave the keynote address at the Democratic Convention."

"Greg, in a few minutes we'll meet the candidates, who will field questions from our moderator, Alexander Morrison, of U.S. Government World News."

The two men looked at their monitor as a camera panned the hall.

"As you can see," said Ellis, "the auditorium is packed for this unprecedented occasion: the first-ever presidential debate between a father and son. Greg, what do you expect to come out of tonight's debate?"

"It's a historic occasion. But more than that, it's no secret there's no love lost between the President and his son. Seems the falling out happened when the younger Winslow publicly announced he was gay some years back. It got stickier when he entered politics as a Democrat. These two men are so far apart on every issue it's almost hard to believe they're father and son."

"Do you think having the debate here in the capital is an advantage for the President?"

"It certainly can't hurt. The latest polls out this morning show Governor Winslow trailing the President by a little more than two points."

"And that's with a margin of error of plus or minus three, is that correct?"

"Yes, it is. Which means—"

"Greg, just a minute," interrupted Ellis. "I see Morrison coming out to take his place at the moderator's table."

Alexander Morrison, in his late sixties, tall with the bearing of a man who knows he's in charge, approached the table, took the microphone, and turned toward the crowd. A two-way wireless earphone was draped over one ear.

As soon as he spoke, the crowd quieted down.

"Ladies and gentlemen. My name is Alexander Morrison and I will be serving as the moderator for this evening's debate. I ask you please, once the candidates have been introduced, hold all further applause until the debate has ended. Also, do not speak or make any sounds during the debate, as such actions may be cause for removal from the auditorium. And now it is my great pleasure to welcome as one of our candidates, the Honorable Governor of the State of California, Bobby Winslow."

As Bobby emerged from backstage and walked to one of the podiums, applause rang out.

"And our second candidate;" said Alexander, "the President of the United States, the Honorable Robert W. Winslow."

Smiling, Robert moved on to the platform and strode toward the second podium. Again, applause came from the audience.

He'd almost reached his place when Bobby approached him, hand outstretched. Grim-faced, Robert hesitated for a moment, gave Bobby's hand a perfunctory shake, then looked quickly away.

"Not a lot of warmth there," Ellis whispered to Greg, covering his microphone with his hand.

"To say the least," said Greg, whispering back.

Backstage, in Convention Room Number One, Wilma, Nate, Ivan, George, Lisa, Wendy, Oren, and Dave had gathered, their eyes focused on the TV monitor.

"Damn!" exclaimed Ivan. "He could have been a little bit more cordial."

"I think we're lucky he didn't ignore him altogether," said Nate.

"Yeah, or give him the finger," muttered Wendy.

230

Back on stage, Alexander sat down, adjusted his earphone, and opened the folder.

"Gentlemen;" he said, "if I may, allow me to state the rules under which this debate will be held."

*****

Alice lay in bed, her eyes closed. Across the room, the TV showed the debate taking place.

Mrs. Carlisle entered the room. "Alice, your son is here."

"Patty?" asked Alice, in a hoarse voice. "Oh, send him in."

"Hey, Mom," said Muhammad, going to his mother's bedside.

"Patty! Oh, Patty, how are you?"

"I'm fine. How're you feeling?"

"Not too good," said Alice. She began to cough.

"You need a drink of water?"

Alice nodded. Muhammad picked up the glass from the nightstand next to the bed. With one hand he held Alice's head up and put the glass to her mouth. She took a sip, then laid her head back onto the pillow.

"I'm dying, ain't I, Patty?"

Muhammad looked away and didn't speak. They both sat in silence.

"How's P.J.?" asked Alice after a few moments. "She coming over?"

Muhammad's eyes grew moist.

"She's fine, Mom," he said, his voice catching. "I don't know; she might be over later."

"Who's that on the TV?" asked Alice.

Muhammad turned to look at the television set.

"It's the presidential debate, Mom; the Governor of California and that dumbass, Winslow—President Winslow."

"Turn up the volume, will you, Honey?" asked Alice, her voice now no more than a whisper.

Muhammad picked up the remote and turned up the volume.

*****

"Mr. President, this question is for you," said Alexander. Last year you authorized our troops to invade Guinea."

"That wasn't an invasion, it was a liberation," said Robert.

"A liberation?" said Alexander.

"A liberation of Christians undergoing persecution, not only in Guinea but in practically every other country in Africa, since 2009. Ever since Obama took office and went soft on Muslims."

*****

"I suppose you'd like to get rid of all of us wouldn't you, you son-of-a-bitch!" said Muhammad, staring at the TV.

Alice roused slightly. "What? Did you say something?"

"No, Mom, just talking to myself."

*****

"Soft on Muslims?" said Alexander.

"You know what I mean;" said Robert, "soft on Muslim terrorists."

"But, sir, didn't President Obama succeed in capturing Osama Bin Landen?"

"Oh, sure, I give him that," said Robert. "But before he did, he started pulling all of our troops out of Iraq, which opened the country back up for other Islamic extremists to take over. Now look at what we have—a terrorist state that has opened up the floodgate for Muslims to begin taking over the whole Mideast, and then Africa."

"But sir," said Alexander, "the Mideast has always been primarily Muslim, at least since the time of Muhammad."

"We were doing something about that under President Bush, weren't we?" retorted Robert. "But it came to a screeching halt under that . . . under Obama."

*****

"Jesus," said Nate, covering his eyes. "Did he *have* to say that?"

"It's what he believes," said Ivan.

"I guess," said Nate, "but did he have to say it out loud—on national TV?"

*****

Alexander shook his head, then continued.

"Back to my original question. We're now engaged in a war not only with Guinea but in essence every other Muslim country in Africa and those in the Middle East that supply that country money, arms, and, in some cases, troops. Do you see any end to this conflict in the near future?"

"End?" said Robert. "Mr. Morrison, it has taken almost twenty years to get to the point where we are now, which is that Christianity is being systematically driven out of Africa. Twenty years ago Christians constituted the majority in countries such as Guinea, Nigeria, and Ghana. There were four hundred million believers in Christ in Africa and a forecast that by 2025 that figure would have reached almost seven hundred million. Do you know how many Christians call Africa home today? Less than three hundred million! We're not gaining—we're losing the continent. At the start of this century, Christians constituted one-third of all the people on the planet. Islam was at twenty percent. Today, less than thirty percent of the world's population is Christian, while almost a fourth is Muslim."

*****

"Is that Robert?" Alice asked, trying to sit up.

Muhammad turned to face her. "Huh? Oh, Robert Winslow? The President?" He turned back to the TV. "Yeah, Mom, that's the murdering bastard."

"Patty, I got to tell you something."

"Yeah, okay, Mom, go ahead."

But Muhammad's attention remained fixed on the TV.

*****

"Governor Winslow," said Alexander, turning to Bobby, "how do you feel about what President Winslow is saying?"

"I'm not sure where the President is getting all his facts. While it is true that Islam is growing faster worldwide than Christianity, there are differing thoughts on whether or not that is true with Africa. In any event, the reason for the growth in Islam is due primarily to the fact that, generally speaking, Muslims are younger than Christians and have a higher fertility rate. So do you invade a country to stop them from becoming too Muslim? Do you slaughter them if you can't convert them?"

"You invade them to stop them from persecuting Christians!" exclaimed Robert.

"No," said Bobby, "I don't think so. You work through the United Nations and through organizations in Africa such as the Economic Community of West African States to stop the persecution. You work through worldwide Christian organizations to provide more missionaries if you want to spread the Gospel. You don't go in and take over a country, tear down their mosques and tell the populace to start worshipping Jesus or risk getting a bullet in the head. That's the extremist Muslim's way of doing it.

"And if it does come to the point where it's necessary to send troops in to protect people, you enlist the help and support of your allies. If Bush taught us nothing else, he taught us that in Iraq."

"That is exactly the kind of tripe I'd expect to hear from a—from someone who doesn't have the—the guts, the fortitude to stand up for what is right," said Robert. "All you namby-pamby, bleeding-heart liberals are the same!"

"You're right," said Bobby. "I am a liberal. And, yes, my heart is bleeding. It bleeds for the poor and the homeless and the disenfranchised in this country who are suffering because so much of our national income is going into fighting this stupid, stupid war. It bleeds for the lives being lost in this totally unnecessary conflict, the brave men and women of our armed forces who are fighting and dying over there, the innocent Guineans who are suffering and dying because we— excuse me, you …" Bobby pointed his finger at Robert ". . . believe Christianity has to prevail over Islam."

Robert's eyes bulged. "Listen, you little—"

"And I promise this," Bobby continued. "The day after I'm sworn in as President, I will initiate the process to begin the withdrawal of our troops from Guinea."

Two-thirds of the crowd rose to their feet, filling the room with applause, whistles, and shouts of agreement that continued for more than a few minutes.

In Convention Room Number Two, Bobby's entourage jumped up and down, pumping their fists into the air.

"Yes!" shouted Hank.

"You tell him, Bobby," cried Annabel.

"That's it! That's it! Give him hell!" exclaimed Kevin.

A far different atmosphere prevailed in the other convention room, where everyone sat quietly, shocked at what they had just witnessed.

"This is not going well at all," said Nate.

Ivan shook his head. "Someone give me a fucking gun, so I can shoot myself."

*****

"Patty, listen." Alice's voice was almost gone. "Robert—the president—he's your real father."

"Okay," said Muhammad dismissively, too engrossed on the scene being played out on the TV to pay any attention to what his mother was trying to say.

"You're gone, you son-of-a-bitch!" he exclaimed when Robert's face came on.

"And he's the one who killed Darren," whispered Alice.

*****

In the auditorium, the demonstration subsided.

"May I ask a question that pertains to the war?" asked Bobby.

"I—I suppose so," said Alexander, not sure how everything had gotten so out of hand.

"Mr. President," said Bobby, "can you enlighten us on Operation Crusade?"

Robert's face turned pale. A stunned look covered his face.

*****

Muhammad looked as surprised as Robert. "What? What did he say?"

"He was a senator then," said Alice. "I was a volunteer worker—"

"Operation Crusade?" Muhammad's brow furrowed.

"I wanted—" Alice struggled to get the words out. "I . . . I just . . . just wanted you to—"

Muhammad grabbed the remote and replayed the previous scene.

*****

"Mr. President, can you enlighten us on Operation Crusade?" Bobby asked again. "You know—your plan to re-Christianize not just Guinea but the entire continent of Africa as—"

"I . . . I have no idea . . ." said Robert.

*****

"Operation Crusade!" cried Muhammad. "That's the story P.J. was working on! Somebody high up in the administration, she said. It must have been him. The President must have been the one she was talking about."

He jumped up from his chair.

"He killed her! That son-of-a-bitch killed her! He had her killed!"

*****

An eighteen-wheeler sat outside the convention center, filled with machinery used to control the TV feed to all the major broadcasting companies covering the debate. Inside, monitors covered one wall. A dozen men and women sat at various control stations.

Spencer Wallman, in charge of the group, covered the earpiece of his headset with one hand. "What? Now? Are you crazy? Okay, you're the boss."

He flipped a switch. "Go to break," he said, speaking into his headset.

*****

Robert, though still rattled, tried to regain his composure. "Where did you—how . . ."

Alexander covered the desk microphone with one hand, turned his head to one side, and whispered into the mouthpiece of his earphone: "What?"

"Go to break," said Spencer. "That's the word from the top."

Alexander turned back to the desk microphone and removed his hand from it.

"I'd also like to know," Bobby continued, "what happened to Norman—"

"Gentlemen," interrupted Alexander, "I've been informed it's time to take a break. Let's say fifteen minutes."

A mixture of relief and anger covered Robert's face.

Bobby looked confused. "Wait—what?"

"Fifteen minutes," Alexander repeated.

Robert hurried from the stage.

Bobby looked around, not sure what just happened.

*****

Muhammad turned toward Alice. "Mom, I've . . . Mom?"

He took Alice's hand: cold. He checked her pulse, and his eyes welled with tears. "Oh, Mom," he murmured.

Muhammad let go of his mother's hand, stood and went to the open door.

"Mrs. Carlisle. Can you come here?

"It's my mom—she's gone," he said when Mrs. Carlisle appeared.

"Oh, I'm so sorry, Patty—Muhammad," said Mrs. Carlisle, moving to Alice's bedside.

"I have something I have to do. Can you call the doctor or 911 or whoever it is that has to be called?"

"Sure. When will you be back?"

"I won't," said Muhammad as he walked out of the room.

CHAPTER THIRTY-EIGHT

In the control truck, Spencer jerked off his headphones.

"Fifteen minutes! What the hell does he expect us to air for fifteen minutes?"

"Take us to a commercial right now," Marcy, Spencer's assistant, barked to one of the technicians.

In seconds a commercial popped up on the main monitor.

"We can't run commercials for the whole fucking fifteen minutes," said Spencer, disgustedly.

"Don't worry," said Marcy. "We can run some tape from their campaigns. Plus, we got some background tape of the governor as a kid, playing with his dad in the backyard. There's plenty more crap like that, too. We'll fill the time."

"I'm going to wring that fucking Morrison's neck when I see him," said Spencer. "Five minutes, maybe. Not a fucking fifteen!"

*****

Seething, Robert waited in the wings, his face contorted in rage. Ivan rushed to meet him.

"That little shit!" said Robert. "Who the fuck does he think he is? I'm going to bury that son-of-a-bitch. Goddamn him! Goddamn him!"

For a moment Ivan was shocked by Robert's language. He'd heard him swear before, but never by taking the Lord's name in vain.

"Okay, look," said Ivan, "he got in a few good jabs. But it's not over yet. We still have the economy to talk about, immigration. Both of those are in our corner, they're areas where the administration has made great strides."

"Who cares? Who the fuck cares? He's brought up Operation Crusade. That's what's on everyone's mind now. That's what they're going to want to hear about; and Norman!"

"Don't let him continue to push on it, then. You push the other subjects, regardless of what question Morrison asks."

"You're right," said Robert. He wiped his forehead with his handkerchief. "I'm the President. I don't have to let that pompous ass set the agenda."

"That's right," agreed Ivan.

"How much time before we start up again?"

Ivan looked at his watch. "Ten minutes."

Robert started to walk away from the stage. "Time enough for a quick drink."

"I'm not sure—"

"Like you said," said Robert, over his shoulder, "I *am* the President. Let the fuckers wait for me."

Twelve minutes later Bobby waited at his podium, studying his notes. Alexander sat at his table and glanced nervously at his watch, then at one of the cameramen, who merely shrugged.

He turned to face the audience.

"Ladies and gentlemen, I trust you have enjoy—"

Polite applause came from the audience. Alexander turned back to see Robert stride onstage. He nodded toward Robert.

"We are back and ready to continue," said Alexander, the tone of his voice betraying his annoyance. "Mr. President, this question is for you."

*****

Outside the convention center, Muhammad tried several doors, to no avail. Rounding a corner, he came upon an armed security guard standing by a door propped open with his jacket. The guard looked up at Muhammad and took a drag on his cigarette.

"Can't smoke inside, huh?" asked Muhammad.

The security guard frowned. "Shit no. Lucky they let me smoke at all."

"You got one I can bum?"

The guard nodded and reached inside his shirt pocket. When he did, Muhammad sprayed him in the face with pepper spray, then snatched the man's gun and struck him on the head. The guard crumpled to the ground.

Muhammad stuck the gun in his belt. Then he picked up the guard's jacket, grabbed the unconscious man by the shoulders, and dragged him into the building, allowing the door to swing shut behind them.

Hoping he wouldn't run in to anyone, he checked several doors closest to the outside door. One was unlocked. He pulled the guard into the room, a small closet, and stripped him of his uniform.

Moments later, Muhammad emerged, dressed in the guard's uniform, leaving the still unconscious man tied and gagged.

He adjusted his cap and headed down the hallway.

When he reached the door to the auditorium where the debate was being held, he waved to the guard standing there, who motioned him in.

Inside, Muhammad hesitated for a moment, then found a position against the back wall and took stock of what was happening.

Alexander was addressing Bobby.

"Governor, we've heard from President Winslow that he feels our nation is enjoying its most prosperous period of time since before the Great Depression, and that whatever poverty and homelessness still exists in our country is unavoidable, an unfortunate state every nation is prone to. What do you think?"

Bobby chuckled. "Unavoidable? Gee, let's see. In the three years since my father took office, federal funding for social services of all types has decreased by twenty-three percent. The poverty level has risen by two point one percent. Four out of every ten agencies that provided assistance to the poor three years ago no longer exist because of a lack of federal funding. Homelessness has increased by over three percent. Why? Because we're not building enough low-income housing. Because most people can't afford four hundred thousand dollars for a new home, which is now almost the national average. And why is that? Because of the high price of construction materials. The President says the economy is booming. He's right about that in one respect. Since he took office our military budget has increased forty-one percent."

"We happen to be fighting a war if you hadn't noticed," said Robert.

"Oh, I've noticed," said Bobby. "We've all noticed. All those people living on the streets have noticed. All those people standing in line to get free meals at the Volunteers of America missions, they've noticed. All the people who are unemployed, waiting in line to receive their unemployment checks—the ones who *aren't* making bombs and drones and guns and ammunition—they've all noticed. Yes, we've all noticed. And the question is: when will this war end? I have the answer; as I said earlier, shortly after I've taken office."

Again, the audience broke into applause. This time Morrison made no attempt to stop them.

"Gentlemen," he said, "I see our time is up. I want to thank each of you for appearing here this evening. I'm sure I speak for all Americans when I say we look forward with anticipation to next week's election."

He turned and faced the camera.

"To members of our television audience, we hope you have found this debate between Governor Winslow and President Winslow both enlightening and thought-provoking. Good night to all."

At the rear of the auditorium, a guard approached Muhammad.

Muhammad moved his hand to his gun.

"What are doing standing back here?" barked the guard. "Get down there to the stage and help control the crowd."

*****

In the control truck, Spencer jerked off his headphones. "Thank God, that's over. Marcy, finish up here, will you? I gotta have a drink."

*****

As Bobby approached his father to shake his hand Robert headed off in the opposite direction. Bobby shrugged, turned, and walked back to where Hank was waiting for him.

On the other side of the stage Wilma, Nate, and Ivan met Robert.

Both groups found their way to the front of the stage and descended the steps to the main floor. Throngs of supporters surrounded their respective candidates, shaking hands and congratulating them.

Muhammad maneuvered his way through the crowd toward Robert.

"Greg," asked Ellis, "what do you make of all this? What do you think Governor Winslow was trying to get in there with his reference to . . . what was it? Operation Crusade?"

"Ellis, I have no idea. It's not something I've heard of before. We have retired General Warren Dutton, chief military analyst for the U. S. Government News Network standing by. Perhaps he can shed some light on this."

General Dutton sat down in a chair between the two newscasters.

"General Dutton," said Greg, "you heard Governor Winslow refer to an Operation Crusade. What can you tell us about it?"

"Greg, I have absolutely no idea what the Governor was referring to. I've checked with several of my colleagues and—"

Muhammad had approached to within six feet of Robert when Bobby happened to glance at him and saw his hand resting on his gun. Muhammad edged closer until he was directly in front of Robert.

"You're the son-of-a-bitch who killed P.J.," he said as he drew his gun.

Acting instinctively, Bobby threw himself at his father, knocking him aside.

The sound of a gunshot overcame the hubbub of noise and conversation.

Bobby crumpled to the floor, blood pouring from his wound.

Wilma's scream rang out through the hall.

Two Secret Service agents pumped six bullets into Muhammad, who slumped to the floor, dead before he hit the carpet.

Robert knelt beside Bobby while a second agent checked for a pulse. The agent looked at Robert and shook his head.

"Oh, God, Bobby," cried Robert, his eyes filling with tears. "Oh, God, no!"

QUINCY'S STORY - CHAPTER XI

Fourteen years had passed since I graduated from Detroit Tech. My last commission to Lieutenant Colonel had come four years ago. In two more years, I would be up for a commission again, but I knew I had risen as high as I was going to.

My role as a double agent had been a low profile one. I'd shared classified information with both sides, none of which resulted in anyone's death, nor any drastic catastrophes. It was almost as if my career in counter-intelligence hadn't mattered much.

That was about to change.

That morning I met with my superior, General Sam Lynch, Deputy Chief of Staff of MI, the Military Intelligence Corps.

"Quincy, I have an important assignment for you, but it's going to be strictly voluntary."

"What is it, sir?"

"The information you've been able to provide us from your contacts with the Taliban has proven to be marginally successful, but we think you'd be a more valuable asset if we inserted you directly into the organization.

"We believe this new bunch that set up shop in Pakistan last year is gearing up for a major attack, possibly on the same scale as 9/11. We need someone on the inside to feed us information. We'd send you on what would be called a fact-finding mission to Afghanistan. Once there, you'd defect and make contact with your source in Kabul. You'd convince them you're afraid you were about to be found out and that you have important information to pass along to their group in Pakistan, and you want to join up with them."

"What information?"

"We'd provide you with something that appears important but actually isn't."

I shook my head. "They're not stupid, sir. Whatever you give me to pass on to them would have to be pretty significant."

"Don't worry about that. It would be."

"When would I leave?"

"Four days from now—next Saturday."

"Can I think about it?"

"Sure. But I'd need to know by tomorrow. Here, I have your transfer papers ready."

The Colonel handed me the paperwork.

"Like I said;" General Lynch continued, "strictly voluntary. If you decide not to go, burn the transfer."

I nodded. "Is that all, sir?"

"It is. You're dismissed."

I walked out of the office, myriad thoughts swirling through my head: Pakistan—was Memona still there? Was she still alive? I'd heard from Richie by way of Faizan that within a year after her father sent her back home she ended up in an arranged marriage.

I'd had no word of her since.

I'd dated several women through the years but never married, although I was engaged once, only because I thought it was the thing to do.

But I'd never forgotten Memona; had never gotten over her. Nor had I ever forgiven her father for sending her away.

As I left the building one thought ran through my mind: if I *did* go to Pakistan, would I try to find her?

On my way home I decided to check out the drop spot where my Taliban handler left me messages whenever he wanted to meet.

It had been more than a month since I'd last heard from him; I wondered if he'd been caught up. But, I figured, if that were the case I'd have heard either at work or from another operative. I hadn't bothered to check the site for a couple of days but with this new possible assignment, I thought I should.

Sure enough, I found the note stuck between two bricks on the side of the building we used for drops.

He wanted to meet me that evening at our normal location.

*****

At five-thirty I was sitting in Lapis, a restaurant in the Adams Morgan area of the District, close to where I lived. Their specialty was Afghan food. I was waiting for the arrival of the Lamb Tikka I'd ordered when I saw him coming toward my table.

For the last year-and-a-half Paywastun was my D. C. contact. I knew from the file we had on him at MI that wasn't his real name, but I never let him know that I knew.

"Cue," he said, sliding onto the seat across from me.

"Pay," I said.

"I have big news," said Paywastun. "I have a new assignment for you—a very important one."

Two in one day? Must be my lucky day!

"What is it?" I asked.

"Let's eat first," he said. "I'm famished."

Paywastun waved the waiter over to our table.

"I'll have the Morgh," he said. "And water."

"How is that?" I asked. "I've never had it."

"It's not Kentucky fried, but it's okay."

I laughed. Paywastun was an easygoing guy, always upbeat, and with a great sense of humor.

We chit-chatted while we waited for our food to arrive. I was anxious to know what this new assignment was, but I could tell Pay was savoring the prospect of telling me, so I played along.

When we finished I pushed my plate aside and looked at Pay.

"Okay, give—what is it?"

"I'm thinking of getting some sheer berenj. How about you?"

"I don't need any damn desert;" I said, quietly enough so only he could hear, "the assignment."

"So impatient. Remember, the Qur'an says, 'Only those who are patient shall receive their rewards in full, without Hisaab'."

I sat back and grinned. "Okay, I'm sorry; at your convenience."

"Actually," said Paywastun, "it's at his convenience."

I turned to see to whom Pay had referred. My jaw dropped—it was Haaziq!

"What . . . what are you doing here?" I asked as he slid onto the bench next to Pay.

"Good to see you, too," he said, flashing those white teeth.

"I mean . . . ," my voice got softer, ". . . how did you get into the country? You're on our watch list."

"Your security needs to be updated," said Haaziq.

"Why are you here?" I asked. "How are you here—I heard you'd been killed."

Haaziq shook his head. "As your esteemed writer Mark Twain once said, 'the reports of my death have been greatly exaggerated.' And, besides, I wanted to give you this assignment personally. I also wanted to see for my own eyes that the soldier I wasn't sure I converted almost twenty years ago was still a convert."

"It's good to see you," I said.

Haaziq reached into his jacket pocket, pulled out an envelope, and handed it to me. "So . . . here is your assignment."

I took the envelope from him, opened it, and removed the slip of paper inside.

As I read it my eyes got big.

"Is this for real?" I asked, looking up.

"Oh, yes," he said, nodding. "It is *very* real. You are very honored."

I sat back, unsure of what I should say next.

"You will carry it out, I presume?" said Haaziq, more a statement than a question.

"It is my duty," I said, folding the paper and replacing it in the envelope which I put in my jacket pocket. My heart was pounding.

Haaziq stood and laid three twenty-dollar bills on the table. "Dinner is on me," he said. "It has been an honor."

Then he walked away.

"Good luck," said Paywastun, sliding off the bench.

I remained for a few minutes, then finished my tea, got up, and left.

QUINCY'S STORY - CHAPTER XII

I'd never been one to have a lot of friends. Growing up in South Central Los Angeles, my circle of buddies always tended to be small. Then, when I joined the army and was transferred from one base to another, the connections I did develop never seemed to travel with me. I could count on one hand the number of close friends I had, including Richie, whom I still kept in touch with, and Shoo.

I'd been living in a nice two-bedroom, two-bath, twelve-hundred square foot condo for the past three years, ever since I was assigned to MI.

I'd met a couple of other people who rented condos in my complex, but about all we had going was a passing "Hi, how are you?" "Fine, how are you?" "Good." exchange of words. All in all, it had been a pretty humdrum life up to now.

Most of my evenings were spent like this one, alone in my condo, watching TV.

". . . and with the preliminary results in from California, we're now ready to declare a winner in the Presidential race."

It was eight o'clock. Normally, networks waited until at least nine to call an election. I knew who the winner was—I didn't need to hear it from the announcer.

I got up, switched off the TV, went into the bedroom, stripped off my clothes, and stepped into the shower. I never liked hot water for my shower—warm was my preference.

When I finished I toweled off and put on the harem pants and tunic I'd laid out earlier and slipped into a pair of sandals.

I walked over to the hall closet and took out the prayer rug I kept there. I'd bought it when I was in school at Detroit Tech, at a small shop on Warren Avenue.

Returning to the living room where I'd been watching the election results, I lay the mat on the floor facing in a southeast direction, removed my sandals, stepped onto it, and began my Isha prayer.

After I'd completed the last part of my ritual, I put my sandals back on, rolled the rug back up, and replaced it in the closet.

I walked into the kitchen, took a bottle of wine from the cupboard, and poured a glass. It was the one vice I was guilty of—a glass of wine in the evening.

I often kidded myself that I must be the only forty-year-old in the world who had never tried an illegal drug—not even marijuana. Heck, I'd never even smoked a cigarette; seeing what it did to my father cured me of any desire to get hooked like he did.

One would think growing up in South Central L. A. among guys who bought and sold and used drugs on a daily basis I would have succumbed somewhere along the way. Or during my time in Afghanistan, when there was nothing else to do I would have bummed a cigarette from one of my fellow soldiers, almost all of whom smoked.

I never did.

But I did enjoy my one glass of wine.

I moved into the study, sat down at my desk, took a sip of wine, and stared at the two sheets of paper there before me, the assignments I'd received earlier that day. I knew carrying out either one meant my life would never be the same.

I picked up the papers, moved them to the side, and opened the journal to the point where I'd stopped last night. I had kept a journal ever since I met Memona, even in Afghanistan. This was the twelfth volume; the first eleven were stored in the safe located behind a print hanging on the wall.

I smiled when I turned the page; it was the last one in the book.

How fitting, that my final entry would find its way to the very last page.

*****

Quincy closed the journal, set it aside, and picked up the book Memona had given him so many years before, the Rubaiyat. As if the book read his mind, it fell open to number thirty-two, his co-favorite poem. He always thought of Memona when he read it.

There was the Door to which I found no Key;
There was the Veil through which I might not see:
Some little talk awhile of Me and Thee
There was—and then no more of Thee and Me.

He sat there, the book resting in his lap. Would things have been different if there *had* been a Thee and Me? If her father had not sent her back to Pakistan? If they had run off and gotten married? They would have had children; of that he was sure. Would they have continued to live in Los Angeles or would life have taken them elsewhere?

He wondered how she was doing? Was she well? Did she love her husband as he was sure she had loved him? Did her husband love her? Did *they* have children?

He sighed.

What difference did any of that make now? She *did* go back to Pakistan, she *did* get married.

The poem was right: there is no Thee and Me.

He picked the book back up and flipped through the pages to what had been his first favorite: number sixty-nine.

He read it out loud.

But helpless Pieces of the Game He plays
Upon this Chequer-board of Nights and Days;
Hither and thither moves, and checks, and slays,
And one by one back in the Closet lays.

And one by one back in the Closet lays.

Quincy closed the book, laid it on the desk next to his journal, turned out the light, and went to bed.

THE FINAL CHAPTER
(one day following the Presidential election)

Several dozen people, including four generals, an admiral, their respective aides, the heads of the CIA, the FBI, the DHS, and the NSA, the Secretary of State, and other White House staffers were crowded into the Situation Room of the White House where they had been patiently waiting for the past ninety minutes for the President to join them.

General Baumgardner paced up and down one side of the room. General Weatherford sat at the conference table and sipped water from the glass in front of him, occasionally refilling it from a pitcher. Admiral Sato and General Lynch sat quietly, Sato's eyes half-open.

General Lynch's aide, Lieutenant Colonel Quincy Bollweber, stood behind him up against a wall.

General Montgomery kept checking his watch.

"If he doesn't—"

Just then Robert appeared. Everyone who had been seated jumped up from their chairs. The others came to attention.

"At ease," said Robert, taking his seat.

"It's time to step up the war in Guinea," said Robert when everyone had been seated.

"Sir?" said General Baumgardner.

Robert leaned back in his chair. "It's time to activate Operation Crusade."

Quincy stepped forward and approached Robert.

Robert looked up at him.

"Sorry, sir," said General Lynch. "This is Lieutenant Colonel Bollweber, my new aide."

"Colonel . . ." Robert started to say.

He stopped short when he saw what Quincy held in his hand.

Releasing the safety lever of the grenade from which he had pulled the safety pin seconds before, Quincy dropped the shell in Robert's lap.

The last voice Robert heard was that of Quincy Bollweber.

"Allahu Akbar!"

ABOUT THE AUTHOR

A retired Lutheran minister, Kenn has served congregations in Indiana, Kentucky, and Missouri. In 2000 he sold his wedding business in Maui, Hawaii, and retired to Lower Northern Michigan (Ernest Hemingway country), where he and his wife, Judy, also a retired minister, both in their eighties, along with their fourteen-year-old dog, Louie, grow gracefully old together, living the good life in their cabin on Deer Lake.